The Bio-Mech War

Book 5: Blue Iguanas

Xavier Therg

The Bio-Mech War

Book 5: Blue Iguanas

Xavier Therg

AOIX
Press

Published by AOIX Press,
An imprint of White Media Works
San Diego, California

ISBN 978-1-64145-026-3

www.xaviertherg.wordpress.com

Other Works by Xavier Therg

Table of Contents

Excerpt from Book 6: Crabb World

Episode 1 – Corridor Rat

The first days of the colony project were like the first days of westward expansion in America. Colonists crowded into creaky, covered wagons and rolled off through hostile environments looking for a patch of land that may not exist. Families were split up and colony ships lost before the black hole technology was perfected. Some of those colonies may have made it, but we'll probably never know. Who goes looking for bones in failed settlements when there were so many promising planets still out there?

With improved equipment and more money rolling in, the colony project became the smooth-operating colony program it is today. Interplanetary colonization could never be made safe, but at least the dangers become routine. Rangers and colonists still got killed but lessons were learned. Each successive graduating class became a little smarter. Unfortunately, many casualties of those lessons were left behind on the moon.

My favorite hunting ground was the three hundred meter corridor leading from the port to Luna City. Colonists arriving after a long trip from Earth were dirty, disoriented, and smelled faintly of vomit. As an orphan of similar description, I blended in easily, bouncing in to grab a suitcase or handbag in the chaos. Even if a colonist saw you taking their stuff, they were just passing through to

Ranger City. They wouldn't stay around to make trouble and keep after security to get their things back.

Another nice thing about colonists, they paid a million dollars each for a ticket. Because they would never go back to Earth, colonists often converted excess fortunes into jewels or gold that they carried in those suitcases or handbags. A good strike could keep me fat for weeks. A thirteen-year-old with a diamond watch tended to arouse suspicion. I had to fence my stuff to even seedier adults for a fraction of their value.

I spotted my target, a harried couple with a kid about my own age. A family this young didn't have time to save three million dollars for the trip. They must have inherited their fortune, and much of it could be in their suitcases. The father looked completely worn out, not that he could catch a spry orphan already living and hiding in the lunar corridors. I slipped into the crowd walking two groups behind.

After days in space even the one-sixth gravity of the moon threw off normal balance. The couple took terrified little hops like they would stick and never be able to move again. The kid loved it, jumping to the ceiling. He had clearly broken any of the couple's pretense at discipline.

After I saw that, I didn't mind so much stealing. If they couldn't even control their kid they were obviously too weak to deserve their stuff. I needed an excuse. My friends among the other orphans were more ruthless, robbing and vandalizing purely for fun. Theirs was revenge against an unjust society. Mine was apologetic survival.

Of the suitcases, backpacks, and briefcase, I targeted the briefcase. I didn't need clothes, and the backpacks were bound to contain snacks and reading material for the trip. The way the father squeezed the handle was telling. Why not tie it to the rolling suitcase?

As they traveled along the corridor, the trio approached the restrooms. It was the first good spot for a grab. They walked past the restrooms but then stopped at a kiosk to check their room assignment. The father held onto the case and typed with his free hand. When I got close enough to hear what the kid was whining about, I heard the word "hungry". The old man couldn't cram his face and hold onto the case at the same time.

The free colonist cafeteria was two floors down, but the woman said, "I see a sign for the Lunesta Café. Last chance for Earth food."

Stem-cell meat and Regolith Cola weren't good enough for rich colonists. They didn't mind spending thirty bucks for a greasy imported ham and cheese sandwich, or sixty bucks for a Coke. Just wait until they were on a colony planet eating leg-of-alien and choking down brackish water. They were soft, comfortable, and bourgeoisie. I had to act quickly. There was no way a corridor rat could get into the Lunesta Café; security would be all over me. What approach though? Knock-and-grab, Helpful Guide, Luggage Porter?

I sprinted to grab one of the free luggage carts, and raced back to catch the family in front of the café. I slicked down my hair. While still behind them, I called out, "Luggage transport! Free luggage transport!" That planted the idea in their minds. Next, a visual. I stepped beside them. "Transport your bags, sir? Ma'am?"

The father nodded to the café. "We're about to eat. I'm sure there are plenty of arrivals who could use your services."

He couldn't just say no thanks. He had to make everyone feel okay about turning me down. That everyone included his wife. I smiled at her and looked at the man earnestly. "Oh no, sir. I'll take them all the way to your room. Be right back with your key before you've finished lunch."

"Oh... um..."

The wife said, "Henry, we don't want to lug all these things into the restaurant."

The man looked more closely trying to detect a scam. "Do you know where R-2216 is?"

"Of course, sir. Three doors from the amphitheater." I didn't know that at all, but I didn't plan on going there. I tried to load the cart. "I'll be back in fifteen minutes." If I could get two bags on, the deal was sealed.

I had to rip a backpack away from the scowling boy, but the man said, "I guess it would be alright, Siff."

Moving more slowly, I felt the weight of each bag and listened to the conversation. The man pretended to read the menu on the wall while the woman talked with the boy, "Siff, did you decide to bring your marbles?"

"I gave them to Steve. I can make some out of river pebbles."

"You're already thinking like a colonist! I'm proud of you!"

"It *will* be a beautiful world, won't it, Mummy!"

"I'm sure it will!"

I couldn't help but snort, disguising it as a grunt as I wedged in the last backpack. I turned to the man to take the briefcase but the father held on to it as he reached into his pocket for a tip. All this work and the mark was slipping away! Of course I could just take the cart to a deserted corridor and paw through the luggage. It would be the smart thing to do, but more than ever I was determined to get the case.

One last chance. Adrenaline flooded my bloodstream as I reached for both tip and briefcase. "Oh, thank you, sir. I'll take this as well."

The man chuckled. "I'll hold on to this. I have some papers to look over during lunch."

"Of course, sir." I pocketed the tip. As the man turned towards the door, I bumped him off balance. While he reached for the cart to steady himself, I twisted the case away and ran for my life.

To cover the shouts as I ran past colonists, I yelled ahead, "Sir! Sir! Your case!"

I ducked into a stairwell and descended eight levels to a deserted, unfinished corridor where I traditionally examined my take. I sat cross-legged on the floor, and held the case in my lap like a Christmas present. My corridor friends preferred an audience but I always savored that moment alone.

The case had no lock; it would only delay the inevitable. I thumbed simple latches, and tossed the papers to my side to look over later. Underneath the folders and a red velvet cloth was what I risked my neck for. Shining like living silver, the Explorer hand blaster was a smaller version of the Ranger's rifle blaster. Nearly as deadly, it had thirty-eight caliber bullets, taser barbs, and two grenades. I hefted it gently, surprised by the mass. On Earth it must weigh six kilos!

I caressed the barrel and looked through the night vision laser sight. I never saw anything so beautiful in my life. And it was all mine! I could fence it and live like a king, but for this beauty I would give up eating for a month. "My precious," I whispered ironically, hugging it to my chest.

It was completely impractical. There was no use for it in the corridors. Of course I could never show it to my friends, but just to hold it now and then would keep my dreams alive with visions of colony worlds.

In the rough rock corridors under Luna City there were plenty of hiding places. I had to hide myself as well. If the case only held gold or jewels, security wouldn't care, but they couldn't allow a hand-blaster loose in the corridors. There would be a search.

I would go to the Laughing Boar. Ex-Rangers hanging out in the bar would hear of any unusual security activity. I could get a meal and wash some dishes, establish an alibi if one became necessary. Before I put the blaster away, I had to try it at least once. Grenades and bullets would be too loud, but the taser was silent.

When I switched on power, the screen inset in the grip blinked immediately. A blaster with a seconds-long booting routine could be fatal. I paged through screens and tested the diagnostics, as proud of the results as if I had bought the thing myself.

I used the night scope to look around the dim corridor. I could mark up to four targets with the laser and press go. The taser would automatically hit those marks within centimeters, until all four barbs were ready for a high-voltage current. Wishing for a rat, I settled on a plastic cup against the wall. The barb connected with a satisfying thwack. When I gave it juice, the cup went flying leaving a trail of flame and smoke.

I polished the blaster all over with the red cloth. Feeling fine scratches along the barrel, I walked to one of the widely spaced corridor lights to read an inscription, "To Henry, fair weather and good hunting. Dad."

So the old man was still alive and didn't make the trip. Very few colony planets were worth it. Why put yourself through death and backbreaking labor when you got millions to enjoy a comfortable life on Earth? It's probably written into the genes, the hunger for excitement. I could see it in the body language of the grizzled, mangled veterans telling stories in the bar. I felt it myself.

I packed the blaster and papers, and buried the case under a pile of rubble along the side of the unfinished corridor. I jogged to make up time, and set my alibi. I could slip into the Laughing Boar and just hang around quietly in back; the owner would think I had been there all day.

Most of the dozen Luna City bars catered to shift workers but the Laughing Boar was busy all day, serving food, drinks, and understanding to ex-Rangers too injured in mind or body to stay in the program. Not that they would let the pain show. With every story of bravado came a pill covertly washed down with whiskey.

I hit the ground with the practiced dive of a corridor rat, rolling under a curtain of beads into the bar. Sitting on the floor in the dark, I melted against the wall, proud to see that not a bead had been disturbed.

I surveyed the patrons, naming them by voice, outline, or position as my eyes adapted to the low light. There were a couple of miners from a nearby settlement but no one to be concerned about. After a few minutes I rose and made my way to the bar. "Hey, Dan," I called to the back. "Any chance for a bowl of rice?"

The bartender clumped out on prosthetic legs like a metal stork. "When did you get here?"

"What do you mean? I've been here."

The bartender picked up a glass and winked. "Got ya'. I guess I could use some help in the kitchen. A new shipload of colonists landed."

I feigned ignorance. "Did they? I guess business will be good for a few days."

"For all of us." He winked again.

"I'll fix you something too," I said, skipping back to the kitchen before Dan's prosthetic eyeball fell out.

I started a pot of rice and cut fish from a meat wall. Dan liked sfish sandwiches with bread grown in the cultured yeast tanks of Mare Crisium. The moon was industrializing as people and resources poured in from Earth for the colony program. Dan called back, "Thuy, steak and egg plates for eight."

The request was so unusual, I brought out Dan's sandwich rather than putting it on the cutout window. "Here you go," I said, peering through dim light. Sitting around a table, colonists were joined by several of the ex-Rangers.

Dan hooked a thumb. "Collies are treating the room to breakfast."

"Steak and eggs? That's a hundred bucks a plate!"

"Can't take it with 'em."

I skipped back to the freezer to dig out pre-cut meat in frosted packages. Checking for expiration dates I separated the hard plastic lumps for defrosting in the microwave. As I took out a carton of eggs and warmed the grill, animated voices rose and fell, occasionally breaking into shouts or bursts of laughter. We didn't get too many colonists in the Boar.

A hearty meal for the condemned seemed appropriate. A year ago I was in their shoes, a rich kid from Earth with no idea how big and cruel the universe could be. Everything was taken away from me, but was my life in the corridors that much different than when I was rich? I woke up, walked around, ate, drank, pissed, crapped, and went to bed, the same as I did a year ago in an expansive estate in Vietnam, the same as the first caveman two hundred thousand years ago.

The only difference was in detail. The poorest person in the world could be the happiest. The richest, most miserable. The poor had only to worry about finding a few small comforts. The rich had to worry about losing theirs. When you're rich, even a new yacht seemed smaller than your neighbor's.

I didn't wish to be poor, but I didn't think about it much either. Since I first started robbing, millions of dollars in wealth passed through my hands. The thought pulled me out of my reverie. I was supposed to be listening for news of the theft. I finished the plates and helped Dan carry them to the tables.

After the plates were down, one of the Rangers grabbed me with a metal claw. "See here! This is what I was talking about. The moon is crawling with 'em."

I growled at the old, black woman and tried to pull free. "Weak as a kitten," she clucked. "After a few weeks of fresh colony air he could swing a pick."

Dan said, "Come on, Selma. Let him get back to work."

The gray-haired colonist asked me, "How about it, son? You want to be adopted and go to a colony world?"

When I stopped struggling the woman let go of my arm. "I've been to a colony world, sir. You'd have to drug me and tie me up before I'd ever go back. You're all going to die."

The black woman shrugged. "Eh, plenty more where he came from. A lot of the orphans were born on the moon. They'd love to go out."

Dan nodded me to the kitchen. As I was leaving, the woman said, "Think of them as sled dogs. They'll pull you through a blizzard, and if things get desperate, you can always eat 'em."

"I don't think I could even eat one of my dogs."

"You'll see, dearie. On a colony world you'll be amazed by what you could do."

I cooked and waited tables the rest of the day. Along with the regulars, two security officers stopped in for a drink. They looked me over before talking with Dan. I stayed in the kitchen ready to bolt through the back door but the officers left after their drinks. I figured I was safe but I didn't return to my familiar tunnels until after midnight.

The tunnels that I and the other orphans inhabited were on the edges of the city. Engineers abandoned the digs because of fractures or unstable geology. After five billion years of asteroid strikes, the moon had a lot of cracked ground. Cracks that leaked air to the surface were sealed but there were plenty of natural caverns for my friends to hide in when they got advanced word of a security sweep.

I wasn't surprised when I found the domiciles of my neighborhood abandoned. Security would know that an orphan stole the blaster. They would come to my camp and a dozen others to ask questions. I chuckled as I crawled into the small crate that I called home. Like the nest of a packrat, my crate was filled with clothing and shiny objects.

A preference for steel left sharp edges for the careless visitor. I stretched out, and with the warm memory of the Explorer in my hands, fell asleep dreaming of distant planets.

Light in the corridor never changed. I had no watch, but I could tell it was morning by the heaviness of my limbs. As I stretched I heard whispers outside my crate. Fellow orphans would never show such consideration, and security would have no need for stealth. I pulled a knife from under the fur jacket I used for a pillow. I wondered if I could disguise the blaster well enough to hide inside the crate, maybe a secret trapdoor under the box.

With a rumbling vibration in the corridor, I peeked out of a crack. My box was slammed from the side and sent skidding down the corridor. My things fell out through the opening, including one of my legs. When the box stopped sliding, numerous hands on my exposed foot pulled me into the corridor.

Hackman still in my grip, I blinked stupidly at my fellow orphans standing in a circle around the box. The oldest of the group named K-line nodded at the knife. "He's got a guilty conscience."

While the other orphans nodded and murmured agreement, I saw the heavy cable-spool they used to knock into my box. There wasn't anyone else but my own family of orphans. "Mooch? What's going on? Sari?"

My own girlfriend squinted suspiciously. "Did you take it, Thuy?"

"Take what? What are you talking about?"

A brutish fellow with the imagination of an asteroid crater, K-line said, "You think you're pretty clever pretending all you got is a knife. Clean it out."

I didn't fight as they dragged me away from the opening. A tiny girl called Shank darted in and heaved armloads of my possessions out the hole. K-line kicked through it, stubbing his toe on a steel novelty. Shank poked her dirty face out the entrance. "All clear, K-line. No blaster."

K-line growled, "What'dja do with it, Thuy? Security took away Ritchie and Superman, and you don't come home all day."

"I was working at the Boar!"

"I know," he smirked. "Me and Mooch came looking."

"For what? A blaster you say?"

"Don't act cute." When K-line nodded, the orphans jumped on me, and knocked the knife away. They must have planned this.

After a scuffle, I was tied with ropes and left sweating on the ground. K-line ran the flat of Hackman's blade along my chest. "Let's see what kind of information your little friend can get."

Fueled by adrenaline I decided quickly on strategy: logic first, absorbing torture, and then the truth. "Look at this logically, K-line. Even if took this blaster, it would be stealers-keepers. Why would I give it to you?"

"See!" K-line crowed. "He's got it!"

Logic was lost on some people. I said, "So you're going to share everything you steal?"

"This ain't money, buddy-boy. It's an Explorer, and we're all suffering because you took it."

There was logic in that, I thought uncomfortably. "So what? Would you keep it for yourself?"

When the other orphans looked at him, K-line replied smoothly, "It would belong to everyone, the whole family could use it."

I underestimated K-line's understanding of power. "So what if *I* kept it safe for the family."

"See!" K-line shrieked. "Give it up, Thuy, or I start cutting!"

"I don't have it!" I yelled, looking for allies in the eyes of the others. How much blood could they stand to see spilled?

With a flick of his wrist K-line opened a cut along my bicep. I screamed and fought the ropes. Blood smeared across the floor. Some of the orphans pulled on K-line's arm, but there was no softening in his expression. If anything, the torture excited him. Had it already gone too far to stop?

Not realizing how much it would hurt, I had to re-think the "absorbing torture" part of my strategy. As K-line knelt beside me, I screamed, "Mooch! Sari! Help!"

One more cut, I thought desperately, gritting my teeth to absorb the strike. *And let it not be fatal.* Hackman descended and then K-line stiffened. He vibrated like a shaken doll. As Hackman clattered to the floor I smelled burning hair.

The security guards handcuffing my orphan clan didn't seem surprised to see me tied up and bleeding on the floor. It only confirmed the subhuman status they held for corridor rats. Nor were my ropes untied. For all the guards knew, I was even lower and more vicious than a corridor rat. At least one of the guards wrapped a bandage around my arm to stop the bleeding.

Orphans knew when to shut up and take it. Guards with taser rifles blocked the corridors while we were handcuffed and led to a security van. As my turn came, I staggered and moaned more than I had to. If a chance to run should suddenly appear, I wanted a startled guard behind me. The first place I'd run to was the unfinished corridor with my blaster. Not that I would take revenge on my family. I had no one else to turn to.

K-line could pay for all of them. As I was helped into the van, I daydreamed about which combination of electricity, bullets, and grenades would be most painful. Handcuffed and sitting on the bench, my best friend Mooch said, "What are you smiling about?"

"Did you really come spy on me at the Boar?"

"For your own good. I wanted to see if security already caught you."

"Why didn't you come in and warn me?"

"K-line stopped me. He said you'd bring the blaster home last night."

"But I don't *have* the blaster!"

"Really?" Mooch searched my face, but didn't say anything more. It was for his own good. Mooch was nice to pal around with but he wasn't the type to keep secrets.

When my family was in the van, the door was slammed shut. I said, "Nice going, K-line. You didn't put out sentries?"

"Shut up, thief, or the interrogation will continue right here."

Sari said, "Thuy's right. We should have stayed away."

In a tiny voice, Shank said, "Wouldn't matter. Something has changed. They'd keep coming back. The blaster may have moved up their plans, but security was planning to get rid of us for good."

Mooch said, "Kill us?"

"No, stupid, back to Earth."

"Wait a minute," I said. "There was a Ranger in the bar last night I didn't recognize, a black lady. She was talking to the colonists about adopting me."

K-line barked an insulting laugh. "Adopt you? They'd wake up with their throat's cut!"

"Look who's talking!" I snapped, rolling my shoulder with the soaking red bandage.

Shank got a hopeful look on her face. "You really think they'd adopt us?"

"Colonists could use the labor and Luna City wants to get rid of us. Maybe the colony program could make a few extra bucks selling us off."

Sari sighed. "A real family! Thuy, do you think we could both be adopted at the same time?"

K-line snorted, "Listen to you suckers! A colony world is a death sentence. No way they're sending me out there as bait. You think a colony family wants to feed you and love you as their own?"

"Not you," I said, getting a laugh.

"That's right not me, and not you either. If we were 'adopted', it would only be to shovel out stables or go see what's rustling in the bushes. I'll smash a window and hop out the Homestead before they ever got me into space."

The orphans were thoughtful as the security van rolled. When the door opened at the shuttle port, orphans thought that their theory had been confirmed. Shank walked up to a guard with a practiced, pitiful look. "Sir, are we going back to Earth?"

"Are you kidding? The free ride is over. You're going to Ranger City."

"Do you mean we're going to be adopted?"

The guard smirked and said no more. We were escorted through the port into an auditorium already half-filled with other orphan families. K-line said, "There must be over two hundred rats here! With a strong leader we could take over!"

I said, "And I suppose you would be the King of the Rats."

"Why not? I'm the biggest and the meanest." K-line squeezed my bandage until I grunted. K-line said wistfully, "If I could only get that blaster out of you."

I kicked K-line in the shin and ran away, setting off a chair-reaction of shoving and cursing. With the uncertainty of the roundup, old rivalries emerged. Security guards swarmed into the seats to break up the worst of the fighting. The commotion didn't completely end until a gunshot exploded at the front of the room.

Orphans on hair-trigger reflexes dove for the seats. Guards seemed shocked as well, but moved slower, looking around in confusion. Eventually everyone faced the same direction, staring at an unshaven, gray-haired man in his early fifties. He had a hard stare and a .45 revolver by his ear pointing towards the ceiling. "Good morning." He didn't shout but his voice carried to every corner of the room. "If y'all would take a seat we can get started."

Orphans climbed from the floor chuckling uncertainly. Guards either took seats or made their way to the walls. "I am Captain Nigel Heard of the Rangers. You are here at my invitation. More specifically, the mayor of Luna City asked me to find a stolen blaster."

My heart beat faster. I was the reason for the sweep. I felt the eyes of my fellow orphans as Captain Heard continued, "Personally, I have no sympathy for a colonist who can't hold onto their things."

Orphans murmur appreciatively; stealers-keepers was the law of the corridor. "But I do have sympathy for the mayor of a fragile city in a harsh, airless world. The blaster must be found. Until it is, none of you will be allowed back into the city."

As orphans looked for escape routes, the Ranger Captain raised a hand. "There aren't enough jails to hold you all, so we're taking you to Ranger City. You will have beds and the run of the city between missions."

Between missions? I had sudden hope, all my dreams of alien planets become reality. All I had to do was keep my mouth shut about the blaster.

Captain Heard said, "Of course we can't just house you indefinitely, so we're starting a new program called the Junior Rangers. Each of you will join one of four groups. When your group is called, you'll get a chance to work alongside the real Rangers establishing colonists on a new world. I can assure you it is a most rewarding occupation.

"Depending on your performance, as you come of age, you will be eligible to join the official Rangers. Security will now distribute color coded wristbands before we board a shuttle for Ranger City."

Orphans were in an uproar as bands of green, red, yellow, and blue were passed around and traded between friends and enemies. I didn't care which group I was in as long as I got away from K-line. Mooch and Sari joined blue team with me while the rest of our quasi-family took green with K-line. I didn't blame them, it was my arm that was bleeding. What kind of leader would I make?

The four teams separated to sit with their group while lunch was brought in. Wristbands were snapped permanently into place and team leaders selected. I wasn't surprised when K-line was picked for green. A natural leader, K-line sat at the front of his team, laughing and learning the names of the few orphans he didn't know.

I only listened with half an ear to blue team leader until Captain Heard again took the stage. He said, "Since no one has yet come forward with information about the missing blaster we'll begin boarding for Ranger City. By the way, the winning team for the coming mission to Stilran-4 is green team."

Red, blue, and yellow teams howled with laughter at green. Although no one knew what to expect, being singled out was enough for derision. The expressions on members of green were divided between sick and excited. As they were heading for the door to the shuttle, K-line screamed and pointed, "It was Thuy! Thuy took the blaster! Take him, not us!"

Face white with terror, K-line tried to fight his way back to the door to Luna City. Maybe it was the fact that his team was going first. More than anything, I felt embarrassed for him. K-line wouldn't be able to show his face among the orphans. Even as they led a babbling K-line away, guards made their way towards me. I sighed and accepted the inevitable.

As orphans were herded to the waiting shuttle, I thought we would just have to turn around and come back again. I could resist the knife of K-line but not the scrutiny of my Ranger heroes. I would give up the blaster.

Outside the auditorium, I was met by the black woman from the Laughing Boar. Dressed in Ranger fatigues, she smiled. "Hello, son. Ready to be adopted by the Rangers?"

"You remember me?"

She pulled a camera eyeball out of the socket. "Photographic memory. Now what's this about a stolen blaster?"

"I'll take you there."

"Where exactly?"

"Level-eight corridor east of the staircase. It's buried under a pile of rubble."

The old woman nodded and said, "So you don't want to be a Ranger?"

"I do! It's all I dream about."

Her throat vibrated silently but no sound came out. It was some kind of communication system. After a minute, the black woman said, "What kind of life is this, robbing colonists and waiting tables in the Boar? You'll love it in the service."

"But I won't be, none of us will. I'm giving the blaster back."

"We'll still take volunteers from among the orphans. I'm putting my career on the line for this program. We just need enough bodies to make a difference. My name is Selma Darling."

While I led Selma and two guards through the corridors of Luna City, Selma told me stories of the planets she's seen. I had heard many of the stories before from Rangers in the Laughing Boar, but I kept quiet as she limped slowly along on prosthetic legs. When we reached my unfinished corridor, I stopped in front of the pile of rocks where I hid the case. "That's odd, I thought it was bigger."

Selma looked at the guards and back. "What was bigger?"

"The pile." I threw stones to the right and left until I was down to bare floor. "It's gone! Someone took it!"

Selma nodded to a guard who took my arm. "Well, son. You've had your fun. Time to get back to the shuttle."

"It's true! I took the case and buried it right here!" I struggled against the guard's grip, looking frantically up and down the dim corridor for another pile of rocks.

As I was led away, I screamed, "That's the cup I hit with the taser!"

A month later, orphans from red, yellow, and blue teams packed the viewing ring at the top of the Lunar Transfer Chamber. It was an agonizing wait through the two-week lunar night and two-week day for the return of the first Junior Rangers from Stilran-4. My team received little training but at least we were starting to think of ourselves as a family. It was amazing how food and a safe environment reduced the cruelest of survival instincts.

Lasers around the walls fired into the center. A sensor pig dropped past us from the ceiling towards the intersection of the lasers, and disappeared as if by magic. Seconds later the Ranger ship Tarantula dropped out of midair, firing thrusters madly as it slammed onto the floor.

An acrid stink of dust and hot air washed to the top of the cavern. Orphans cried out in surprise. That was dust and air from another world! Right away we could see something wrong. Emergency teams rushed from the doors hauling stretchers across the floor. The Tarantula's damaged engines were still smoking as hatches banged open. Bodies were passed out of the hold and rushed away followed by limping survivors. Junior Rangers looked like nervous battered chickens after a storm.

Sharp-eyed Sari pointed. "There's Shank!"

Rangers in tan jumpsuits climb out and then all too soon the Tarantula was empty. Selma looked up at the orphans high above, giving a salute. Mooch said, "I count nineteen Junior Rangers. How many went on the mission?"

"Thirty-two," I said.

"Maybe some of them were adopted and stayed on the planet."

"Yeah, maybe," I said, dying to talk to green team survivors. "Let's get back to our tunnels."

Sari said, "Thuy, I didn't see K-line."

"Yeah, I know, but all the Rangers made it." Maybe K-line was right, Junior Rangers were run out front to draw alien fire. I shrugged in resignation. Every country on Earth did the same thing, sending young men to fight useless wars. At least with the colony project they were trying to build something.

Sari said, "I wish they hadn't sent K-line back to his team. They probably killed the snitch themselves."

Four weeks later it was blue team's turn. Mooch, Sari, and I joined twenty-eight other orphans strapping into small coffins lining the walls of the Tarantula. In case of a crash, Junior Ranger bodies would provide cushioning. Rangers sat in the protected middle of the ship complaining about the stink as Junior Rangers vomited or otherwise disgraced themselves inside their coffins.

I nearly barfed myself as the Homestead rocked like an ocean liner, rising to the top of the Lunar Transfer Chamber. From my spot near the front I could see out the pilot's window. Red and yellow teams stood around the viewing ring with survivors from green. It was rumored that after the first round of missions, Junior Rangers would be sorted into new teams. Would it be four smaller teams, or three large ones?

The Homestead hovered like a living creature as energy flowed from the solar ring to massive capacitors that fed the lasers. At a switch, all that energy was released. Like a dam breaking, the lasers fired. The Homestead fell while a lumpy fold of space clicked two distant pieces together. The Transfer Chamber brightened in the skies of an alien world. Orphans around me screamed or cried while nervous Rangers yelled at them to shut up.

The Tarantula swooped off the back of the Homestead to scout a landing spot. I caught glimpses of mountains and green forests. I gathered more from the Ranger's conversations. After an hour the Tarantula returned to a tidal plain on the coast near the headwaters of a river. A marsh would provide a softer landing for the Homestead.

The Tarantula dropped onto the ground nearer the trees. Rangers tense while orphans relaxed. The flight itself held more terror for Junior Rangers than any stupid planet with rocks, trees, water, and animals. Instruments in the skids tested air, water, and soil samples. Four-legged rats with heart monitors were run out to check for predators and then finally the two-legged corridor rats as a final check for danger.

Mooch, Sari, and I huddled by the open hatch while other members of blue team wandered over open ground touching alien plants in wonder. The sky was gray with clouds piling on the horizon over a flat ocean. The Junior Ranger team leader said, "Alright, you got your collecting bags and specimen jars. Spread out around the ship and stay in sight."

The human voice sounded almost sacrilegious in the heavy, still air. Mooch whispered, "Hey, Thuy, you want to go check out the forest?"

Armed Rangers emerged from the hatch of the Tarantula. I said, "Okay, just don't turn your back to the trees."

As we walked over the ground, Mooch kicked at loose pebbles. I watched my feet for burrowing insects. For all the difference of this world, we might be in a rice village in my native Vietnam. Was life really created in the same basic forms all over the universe? Chemical reactions on Earth operated with the same exact forces of repulsion and attraction between electrons, protons, and neutrons.

Sari bent over, brushing at a circular, plate-sized depression in yellow mud. "Look at this, there are holes around one side."

I spread my fingers to put in some of the holes. "Guys, back to the ship!"

Mooch frowned. "What is it? We're almost to the trees."

Another trio of Junior Rangers were already into bushes at the forest edge. I called out, "Kevin, Frank, Susan, get back here!"

As Kevin waved, a dark mound of hair fell out of a tree. Like a Grizzly bear, the creature crushed Kevin and Susan under its mass. Frank was knocked to the side screaming. Junior Ranger sample parties picked up the cry.

Shots rang out before the creature could raise its head. One end of the beast turned into a fountain of orange foam. Selma stood on top of the Tarantula scanning the trees through the sight of a hand blaster.

Along with the rest of the Junior Rangers, I staggered back to the ship. Selma said loudly, "Well, dears, what did you expect? A picnic? Drop your samples off and get back out there."

I wondered how many would comply? I wondered if I had the guts myself? Sunlight glinted off fine lines along the barrel of Selma's blaster. As I walked closer, I was sure it was the one I stole from the colonist. Selma must have sent guards ahead when I revealed the location.

She turned her eyes from the forest to give me a quick wink. "Welcome to the Junior Rangers."

Episode 2 – Splashdown

[Two years later.]

My name is Thuy. I have black hair chopped short and quiet brown eyes. I'm Vietnamese, one point six meters tall and weigh forty-four kilograms. If you passed me on the street you would never guess that I know twenty-three ways to kill a man with my bare hands. It's my job to prepare for the unpleasant. I'm the survival expert in a team called the Junior Rangers. Six times a year we're sent to near parts of the Milky Way galaxy to help settle colonists on new worlds.

The planets we find aren't pictured in *Better Homes and Gardens*. They're rough, dark, and dangerous. The twenty-three ways I could kill a man may not apply to a spitting orange snake but every creature has to breathe. Every creature can be made to bleed. A voice appears inside my head, [Hey, Thuy, I told you to meet me at the Doc-in-a-Box.]

I form words silently in my throat, which is called coding. The stack register translates movement of my tongue and throat, sending the words to a radio in my friend's jaw that only he can hear, [Right behind you.]

As Siff turns, my feet catch him beside both ears lifting him sideways into a wall. It's a neat trick, even in the one-sixth gravity of the moon. Siff shouts and tries to pry my bare feet loose from his head. I said twenty-three ways with my bare hands. Bare feet add another fourteen lethal possibilities.

The self-proclaimed leader of the Junior Rangers steps into the corridor behind us. Ivan shakes his head as Siff and I wrestle on the floor. "Big surprise, two morons squabbling like idiots."

I let go of Siff and stand up. With a dignified bow, I say, "The knife must stay sharp."

Siff rubs a red ear. "What'th eating you, Ivan?"

"We jump in one hour. Black hole won't wait. Get your meds, comrades, and finish loading Dragonfly."

"You're not my thupervithor."

Poor Siff. Although he doesn't remember, I met him two years ago when his family was headed to a new world. That is, I swiped a hand-blaster from his father. Siff didn't lisp at the time. I've heard of some of the horrors he faced on Stilran-4, and he was mentally damaged when he came back. I try to protect him now. I've always wondered if his family could have been saved if they had kept that blaster?

I pull Siff's arm to the window, remembering suddenly that I'm excited to be here. The medical technician says, "Leeches please."

We unbuckle leather bands, and drop leeches onto the window counter. The inside of my wrist shows razor bite marks where the leech tests my blood or delivers medicine. On an alien world the leech checks for signs of infection. Ivan rubs at the itchy scratches on his wrist, growling, "Don't I got enough pain in my life already?"

Siff usually codes to save the embarrassment of talking like a baby. [The engineer for Charlie team?]

"How did you know? Did she say something?"

I say, "Not too many secrets in a one industry town. What's her name... Tella?"

"You *know* it's Terra!"

"Well, you're in luck. They're adding a chemical to the leech reservoir, a supercharged pain killer."

Siff clucks his tongue. [Without that dull ache inside, Ivan would never ask her out.]

"What would you know of love, chicken?"

While smiling innocently at Ivan, Siff codes to me, [What a sourpuss.]

"First one," the technician says, laying my leech on the counter.

I fling it around my wrist and secure the buckles. [Leech, activate.] Needles bite into my skin in a scrabbling motion.

Siff says, [Any difference?]

"I'll check." I put on my projected optic goggles, pogs for short. A transmitters sends data dirctly to the optic nerve. I code, [Leech, inventory,] and a list of medicines appears in the air before me. "There it is. Stack, audio data on Gravitol."

From my wrist, the stack register says, "Gravitol, a powerful anesthetic delivered intravenously. Gravitol stops pain by blocking CF-5 receptors on sensory neurons. Approved for standard issue on colony missions, Gravitol is manufactured by Pharmaco Industries and is featured in the slogan, 'Let Gravitol pull your pain away.' First synthesized by Jerry..."

"Stack, stop data."

Siff gets his leech back. While he buckles it on he says, [There you go, Ivan, let Gravitol pull your pain away.]

I brought a needle for the occasion, pressing the point to the pad of my finger. I go slowly to give the leech time to react and then press harder. Where it burrows into the sub-layer, punctured cells release frantic chemical messages. Nerve endings pick up the call and signal to my pain centers.

Siff says, [Hey, slow down there, buddy. What are you doing?]

At the first sign of pain my body instinctively fights to jerk the needle away. I pause long enough for Gravitol to go to work. The pain fades to an ache and finally to stiffness. The needle emerges from the other side of my finger pad, pushing before it a bright spot of blood.

[Sick,] Siff says admiringly.

Ivan only shakes his head. "Wipe blood off hand, and wipe smile off face. Is magic trick. I might give Gravitol to colonists but I expect more from Delta Ranger. A survival expert must use pain, not eliminate it. If you go numb out there on planet you're going to make bad decisions. Pain is tool, information your body needs. Don't close mind to what it tells you."

"Whose mind is closed? If pain is controlled I'm more in charge than ever." Sawing the needle back and forth proves my point, as well as making a mess.

The stack watch of every colonist and Ranger announces, "One hour to Event."

Siff hands me a napkin. [Come on, buddy, we still got work to do.]

Ivan smirks as we walk away. I code to Siff, [You know what I'm talking about, right?]

[Of course. You get a headache, take an aspirin. It's no use trying to think when your head is pounding.]

[Exactly!] I code, but Ivan's criticism stings. As a survival expert I must be completely in tune with the environment, brain and body working together. How can I remain alert if my body's complaining? No, Ivan's just being Ivan. When Rangers aren't around, it's Ivan's job to make us miserable. I'll return the favor, maybe anonymously send him a heart-shaped cake.

Siff and I reach the Lunar Transfer Station, the massive cavern sunk into the crust of the moon. At the bottom of the cavern sits the colony ship Homestead XXVI. All colony ships are named Homestead, the Roman numeral twenty-six indicating mission number. How many colonists still live on those first twenty-five worlds?

On the back of the Homestead perch two little insect ships Black Widow and Dragonfly. The Rangers ride in the Black Widow and the Junior Rangers in the Dragonfly. When the mission is over the Widow and Dragonfly hook together for the trip home.

The Homestead and all the technology packed inside stays behind with the new colony. Rangers never go back to check on a colony. It costs way too much. Once they're in place, colonists are on their own to fade or thrive as best then can. Light-years from Earth, it'll take decades just to receive the first progress reports by radio.

Siff and I take an elevator to the cavern floor and navigate an obstacle course of fueling hoses snaking across the ground. Nervous colonists stand around the loading port, some laughing, some crying. They're leaving Earth forever. My parents and I were colonists four years back when our ship was attacked by alien kangaroos. Half the colony was wiped out, my parents among them. I was brought back to Luna City an eleven-year-old orphan.

I prowled the corridors of Luna City with a lot of other orphans, doing odd jobs and stealing when I had to. The moon is a harsh environment with two straight weeks of minus two hundred degree nights followed by two straight weeks of two hundred degree days. Airless vacuum is only a few thin walls or leaky seals away. The miners, pilots, technicians, and mechanics that came to launch the colony program had dangerous jobs. They were well paid and liked to drink. The combination left a lot of broken homes and forgotten children.

However we got there, it was too expensive to ship us home. Orphans were tolerated as long as we weren't too big a nuisance. Every election cycle, politicians railed against "the orphan problem". No one did anything about it until I committed the one unforgivable crime, stealing a hand-blaster. Luna citizens wanted us gone.

The Ranger Captain at the time realized that orphans were free, and small enough to fit into tight spaces. No one would complain if we got killed. Using my crime as an excuse, security guards swept Luna City corridors for orphans. Like eighteenth century British commoners we were pressed into service as "Junior Rangers". I blame myself for the program, and all future tragedies befalling my fellow orphans.

Colony planets ate us up like popcorn shrimp. Even Rangers got a twinge of conscience. When Captain Heard got killed on Freemount-2, a new policy was instituted. Before being turned loose on an alien world, Junior Rangers were given training, blasters, and a ship of their own. Captain Stiles was a hero to us expendable minors. Unfortunately, Stiles lived only a few missions but the policy stuck.

Since Captain Stiles tenure, the loss of Junior Rangers is no greater than the rate for regular Rangers. I think they resent this for some reason. I've overheard Rangers talking about the good old days when they didn't bother learning the names of Junior Ranger. They were different every time. My family.

I feel teary as we reach the Dragonfly and find Crystal and Anacine getting ready for jump. They're orphans too, Anacine the latest arrival to the program. I'm the only one left from the original group. All those laughing, crying faces, exploding briefly into existence and just as quickly fading into galactic dust. A lucky few were adopted into families on colony worlds. Most went to fill alien digestive systems.

Standing by her locker, Crystal says, "Are you crying, mon?"

"Of course not!" I snap, wiping my eyes. It must be a side effect of the Gravitol.

Crystal shrugs and turns back to a locker full of spare arms and legs. Crystal is a Link, a human with mechanical parts. I sometimes call her Tinkertoy but not too loudly. She's surprisingly sensitive and those arms could crush a car.

Anacine says to Siff, "Where's Ivan? Terra is bringing Ping over. She wanted to say hi."

[Oh really?]

Siff likes Anacine and vice versa. Instead of doing anything about it, they gossip about other couples. It's their way of flirting. Siff says he doesn't believe in office romances but I think it has more to do with Anacine's gills. Stretched across her collarbones, the gills let her breathe underwater but they do give her a "creature" look.

One official Ranger sometimes travels with Junior Rangers in the Dragonfly, a female porpoise named Ping. Her official title is Second Engineer for Charlie team but the job title is more for bookkeeping. She got the job because she can swim.

Charlie team's First Engineer, Terra, brings Ping on a cart. She looks around as we load the porpoise into her traveling sling. Terra waits for Ivan until our watches announce, "Twenty minutes to Event." She nods goodbye and ducks out looking worried.

Siff codes to me, [Not like our pilot to be late.]

[He turned off the auto-tracker in his register.]

Before we can notify the Rangers, Ivan strolls in whistling. As he heads for his seat we put on pogs and check preparations a final time. Not that we could run out and retrieve anything we forgot. Rain falls whether we're home or not.

"Ten minutes to Event."

The Homestead's engines cycle. Vibrations shake the massive beast below us. Bolted onto her back the Dragonfly rattles like a cube of ice in a glass. Sitting in the copilot seat, Crystal says, "By the way, Ivan, Terra stopped by."

"Oh?" Ivan says, and nothing more. Junior Rangers make kissing noises at each other as we belt in for the final countdown.

When Ivan doesn't respond, Anacine shrugs. "Lover's quarrel."

The Homestead lifts off inside the cavern, rising slowly to the ceiling. Outside in the lunar crust a gigantic superconducting ceramic ring spins electrons around and around. They've gathered speed and energy through the last two weeks of lunar daylight. When a switch is thrown they're dumped into lasers ringing the cavern.

As gaseous iron atoms are crushed into a singularity, a miniature black hole opens below us, the gravitational force causing two folds of lumpy space to stick together. Instead of traveling years to another planet we take a shortcut. From our lunar cavern the Homestead falls into an inversion space, and because we design the black hole precisely, it falls into the sky of another world.

One second we're on the moon, the next we're falling into the cloudy skies of a planet light years from Earth. Back on the moon, solar panels will be in darkness for the next two weeks. For two weeks after that the panels will be in daylight spinning electrons faster and faster until once again they power the lasers to build a black hole again and bring us home. We have exactly twenty-eight days to decide whether our colonists will ride back with us or stay on this planet forever.

I can decide in seconds. The planet is a beautiful blue ocean world with ice cap poles and green islands scattered around the equator. Our colonists found a tropical paradise. Despite my expert opinion, Rangers go to work gathering data and looking for flies in the soup.

The planet is small with a gravity a little over half of Earth's. I like a low gravity, easy on a body and it's fun being able to jump three meters into the air. There are no mountain ranges or oceanic rifts. In geologic terms, it's a dead or inactive planet. This doesn't mean absence of life, only that continental plates are stuck in place.

The sun Klondike looks much bigger in the sky than Sol, like a harvest moon but it's hidden by clouds much of the time. Landmasses are distributed evenly around the globe, a chain of islands that circle the equator. A minor tilt in Klondike-2's axis reduces the variations in seasons to almost nothing. It's a timeless world with day following day always the same for billions of years.

The Homestead fires engines and sweeps through the sky. We look for a landing site, having a choice from among a dozen major islands the size of New Zealand and hundreds of smaller ones the size of Hawaii. Anacine's eyes mist over like she's sailing home. "It's beautiful."

Crystal says, "Careful, girl. You'll drop saltwater tears in your gills."

"At least I won't rust."

Siff says, [A billion cubic kilometers of ocean to swim.]

Ping struggles in her webbing anxious to get out and explore. The stack register translates her squeals to our watch radios, "Down, down new water."

The Homestead releases positioning satellites and drops instruments to search for signs of life. It's obvious even from sixty kilometers in the air. The islands have the lush green color of chlorophyll, or rather a Klondike-2 version of chlorophyll. Crystal loosens the straps on her shoulders. "With all that green we'll have plenty of vegetation to burn for energy."

Ivan says, "Want to bet Homestead lands in water?"

"Our colonists don't got gills. You're on. What do we bet?"

"Car wash for Dragonfly if I win."

"Complete overhaul of my limbs if I win, all of them."

The Homestead circles lower dropping to ten kilometers. We've rounded the globe twice already and have enough data. As we head for a piece of land shaped like a horseshoe, Crystal smiles. "Got you, mon. *Fantasy Island* beats *Waterworld* every time."

Ivan holds up a hand for silence as the Captain's voice sounds from the Dragonfly's speakers, "Ladies and Gentleman, this is Captain Wallen. Thank you for your patience during the planetary survey. We chose a landing site in the protected bay of the island below us. We should splash down in about twenty minutes."

Ivan says, "And don't forget hot wax."

"You cheated!"

Ivan is silent behind his pogs. He must have a spy inside the Homestead's control room.

There's a knock on the belly hatch. Anacine smiles at Ivan. "No escape now, loverboy."

Anacine opens the hatch, and Li'l Mike climbs up into the hold. "Doc Blaitel said I should stick with Junior Rangers this mission."

Siff groans, [I thought you were going with the Rangers?]

"Orders. What am I supposed to do?"

We accept the inevitable despite the trouble Li'l Mike has caused. We're all under orders: mechs, Junior Rangers, Rangers. Somewhere on top there must be *someone* pulling the strings. Anacine pats the seat next to her. "Hop up and put on your belt."

Crystal looks back. "Li'l Mike, where did you just come from?"

"The control room. Didn't Ivan tell you?"

"I knew you cheated!"

Ivan stares straight ahead, "Bet is bet. Hang on, comrades. We're going to drop Ping to check for hazards in bay." Ping thrashes her tail in anticipation and lets out a dry blat from her blowhole.

The Dragonfly is held onto the back of the Homestead with explosive bolts. Ivan triggers the charges, and cloudy skies spin around our windows. We swoop over the side and dive. We're used to Ivan's flying. I think I could eat a bowl of rice on a roller coaster by now.

The island looks more and more like a continent as we get closer, and I can see why the water landing. The green of the island is a forest, the mother of all forests. Trees everywhere tower hundreds of meters above ground level. There's not a break in the cover anywhere in the whole wide canopy.

Siff whistles. [It's just not possible!]

Crystal says, "Ivan, you got a radar fix on those monsters?"

"Thousand meters at beaches rising to two thousand in middle."

We're not exactly low over the water but trees on the beach tower over our heads. I say, "Those are like three-hundred story buildings on the beach!"

Ivan says, "And six-hundred story buildings in middle. It's wonder what low gravity will do for tree."

"Not gravity alone. What about storms or fire? These forests are unnatural."

Crystal says, "Let me out, mon. I'll find out why."

Ivan says, "Not our mission. Get cables on Ping. You can take her down with Anacine but don't go in water."

"I just might slip."

The Dragonfly skims around the bay taking readings off the ocean floor and looking for a place to drop Ping. I point out the window. "Ivan, delta fan at three o'clock."

Under the water a formation of dirt and rock spreads out like a "V" from the forest edge. It marks the headwaters of a river flowing out from the forest, and a break in the trunks where they separate over swift moving water. The trees close up again very low over the river leaving only a narrow dark tunnel of air.

Ivan thumbs the radio. "Captain, are you watching? We got river on north bank, looks to be fairly major. Thirty meters wide at mouth."

"Roger, Dragonfly. Drop a water tester along with Ping. We'll bring the Homestead down as close to the river as we can get."

Siff says, [Hot dog! Trees to burn and clean water. We're on vacation.]

Crystal makes a voodoo sign of protection. "Don't jinx us, mon. We've never found a planet yet that didn't throw up nasty surprises."

[Leave the surprise for my birthday.]

Crystal is part of Bravo team responsible for finding a source of energy. Siff is Alpha that finds an on-planet source of food. Anacine is Charlie that finds clean water, I'm part of Delta that provides security, and Ivan is Echo to provide transportation. All teams equally important, we couldn't stay if any resource is shortchanged, energy, food, water, security, movement. Of course security is a top priority before any of the others get to work. I like to think of us Deltas as first among equals.

The Dragonfly extends rotors so we can hover and dart over the water like the insect for which she's named. Ivan brings us close to the beach. Green leaves high overhead push towards sunlight. Below the canopy it's dark with mottled, twisted trunks, looping vines, and a crusty muck oozing out at the base and along the banks.

The river that flows out of the forest appears to be clean. Because the forest is so old, as in thousands of years for trees to get that tall, the water must be pretty clean. If the river is still carving out mud the trees would have nothing to stand in. We swing Ping out the door on a crane, lowering her to the swift moving water running out of the trees.

At the junction between fresh and saltwater Ping will be a little safer. Fresh water creatures will stay in the forest and saltwater creatures further out to sea. The interface is a shifting ecosystem with hopefully fewer defenders.

Anacine and Crystal ride the cable with Ping. Anacine cradles a blaster under her arm peering fiercely into the water. Crystal has her saw blade hand. We leave Li'l Mike safely belted in his seat while I ride on one landing skid with my blaster set on taser. Siff rides the far skid with bullets. The Dragonfly can swim as well. At the first sign of trouble Ivan can cut the cable loose and dive leaving Junior Rangers to swim or drown as we choose.

The entire colony watches through the Dragonfly's belly cameras as Ping splashes in her webbing and swims free. She takes a few quick leaps and heads down, fat tail pumping with the thrill of new water.

Our watch speakers click as she sounds out terrain. Squeals are translated by the stack, [Water clean good. Smell fish.]

[Don't eat,] Anacine warns needlessly. Porpoises don't actually have noses, but they "smell" through chemical receptors in their mouths.

[Bottom soft, sandy. Deep river mouth. Ocean deeper. Steep, deep deep bottom.]

Ivan says, "Homestead, you copy?"

"Roger, Dragonfly. Coming down on top of you. Suggest you move east at earliest possible convenience."

Ivan codes to the Junior Rangers, [You heard 'em. Ping, swim east and stay in visual. Acknowledge.]

[Okay.] Ping knifes like an arrow for the eastern bank of the bay.

Ivan codes, [Crystal, Anacine, reel up cable and everyone get inside.]

The Dragonfly sways as the cable lifts the girls off the water. I look down and almost shout. There are three bodies on the sling! I look again and then code privately, [Siff! Look down!]

Siff walks to the open hatch to see Terra riding the cable with Crystal and Anacine. He winks at me and then looks over his shoulder at Ivan. I'm not sure if it's a good idea startling our pilot, but this is almost worth the risk. Will they continue their quarrel inside the hold?

Terra's face appears in the hatch. I can't read her expression as she climbs inside. Like a psychologist I look back and forth hoping to catch both Ivan and Terra's reactions when they see each other. When Terra clears her throat I settle on Ivan. He looks over and blinks. A gleam seems to come into his eyes like a fighter hearing the bell.

Ivan calmly reaches over and puts the Dragonfly on auto-hover. He undoes his seatbelt and walks back. Without a word he takes Terra in his arms. I look at Siff and shrug as Crystal and Anacine scramble into the hold around them.

Anacine walks over to Siff and *they* start hugging! It's catching! When I look at Crystal, she says, "Don't even think about it, mon."

"Not me! I just don't understand." I look at Li'l Mike. "How about you?"

The mech shrugs as well. Nice to know I'm in good company. When I continue to look confused, Crystal says, "The Black Widow dropped Terra off to check out the ocean."

"I understand that." I point to the two couples. "What's *this*?"

"Breaking and reforming a bond makes it fit better, makes it stronger. Every relationship needs fine tuning."

Terra pulls her head back. "I brought Ping but you weren't here."

"I was running late." Ivan's voice is hoarse.

"Mind if I stay until the Homestead is down?"

"As long as you want."

The speaker announces, "Dragonfly, is there a problem?"

Ivan skips back to his seat holding Terra's hand. As they take pilot and copilot chairs, Ivan hits the radio. "Sorry, Homestead. We're moving."

While the rest of us belt into our seats we check the roof camera as a billion kilo beast falls towards us like a whale on a bunny. The bay is wide, two kilometers across. We move towards open ocean and green forest arms encircling the bay in a hug. Even in low gravity the Homestead has little control with stubby wings. She drops on a steep angle firing retrorockets madly. Hopefully we'll get the colony set up at the forest edge, and those rockets will never fire again.

As the Homestead hits water, geysers of steam and fog spray a hundred meters into the air. A tidal wave rolls into the forest bringing out slushy walls of mud, and turning the aqua blue of the bay to brown. Further out in the water Ping has the time of her life riding the pounding currents. It'll take hours for particulates to settle. Humans have arrived on Klondike-2.

Will our colonists be absorbed into the forest, leaving only mysterious bones and artifacts for alien Klondike archaeologists? Or will the colony build towns and cities, and spread to other islands? With a little luck, Klondike-2 could become another Earth with cities and traffic jams.

Episode 3 – The Terrace

The Homestead nudges into a beach, with a freshwater river as her front porch. Trees from the forest reaching impossibly high overhead, and swampy mud at the roots hug the Homestead's side like mud cupping a river-smooth rock. Colonists don't pour out hatches to climb trees or fish the banks. It will be hours before scientists finish testing for dangerous viruses, bacteria, plants, animals, and chemicals.

While colonists wait, Junior Rangers get a head start. We fly around the island taking video of everything. We drop Terra back into the water, and as we investigate dark corners of the bay, the Black Widow lifts off the back of the Homestead, flying off over the trees on a mission. We wear pogs to keep track of data pouring in from science teams. As part of Delta team, a list of security issues floats in front of my face. "Hey, Siff, they're finding animals."

[Some are already in the lab. Doc Blaitel is checking them for protein compatibility with the meat walls.]

Ivan says, "We've identified five major ecological niches: ocean, river, canopy, forest floor, and mid-level."

Crystal says, "I know the first four. What's a mid-level? Sounds like a corporate bean counter."

"Trunks rise two thousand meters between roots and leaves. Most of forest is dark mid-level."

Siff says, [Can you get us through the canopy to look?]

The Dragonfly heads up along the forest contour, searching for a break in overlapping branches. Trees come in varieties and colors from lime to deep blue-green. They all have wide flat leaves to soak up sunlight and crowd out neighbors. Vines and fungus-like sponges drape from thicker branches to feed off marrow of the trees.

We haven't seen feathered birds but there are sailing creatures, part reptile, part bird with scaly legs and webbed wings. About the size of a squirrel they scamper along a branch and jump. With webbing extended they glide to lower branches. I doubt they'd have the strength to fly long distances or from island to island. As the Dragonfly approaches the wall of trees, flocks of these little sailers flee before us. Ivan says, "I see no way into trunks. I'm going to blast hole."

Crystal says, "You'll set the whole forest on fire, mon!"

"Bullets only. Unless trees are made of metal, forest should be okay."

As if approaching a kilometer tall building, the Dragonfly edges up to the wall of green. Ivan gives natives time to scatter and then points the gun barrel into the center. Bullets crunch through leaves and wood in a storm of flying splinters. The Dragonfly moves in a slow loop carving out a circle. Surprisingly, many of the bullets ricochet backwards like they *are* hitting metal. Ivan backs up to make us a smaller target and continues firing.

Waves of panic spread through the ancient forest, but Ivan's technique is effective. After several minutes a tunnel is clearly visible through the green into a dark twisting interior of interlocking tree trunks. Ivan shines a spotlight through the tunnel. "Now to expand opening to clear Dragonfly's blades."

Before he gets started a voice sounds from our watch speakers, "Junior Rangers, this is Captain Wallen. Return to the Homestead for assignment."

Crystal says, "We're breaking into the mid-level."

"We can hear that all the way back here. We have a less destructive method. You're going to swim through the river and climb up to the mid-level from the inside."

Anacine says, "I bet all the action's in the water. There's no food or water in the dark insides. Mid-level tree trunks sound about as interesting as a sand dune."

Ivan says, "I'll drop you off at river and come back to work on tunnel."

Li'l Mike says, "Anacine, could I come with you?"

Noticing the mech's hand on her knee, Siff says, [Forget it.]

Li'l Mike drawls, "I don't think that's for you to say."

[Excuse me?]

Li'l Mike holds up his hands, palms forward. Siff laughs nervously, [What does that mean?]

When tiny needles thwick out of the mech's hands, Siff actually looks frightened. Li'l Mike says, "I can climb trees without a rope. Shall we call Captain Wallen?"

[Whatever. Just stay out of the way.]

Li'l Mike squints at him and retracts the needles. I must say the whole group feels a little uncomfortable.

Our exploration party consists of the Charlie Rangers, Serena, Terra, and Ping, the Delta Rangers, Thor and Rocky, the Junior Rangers, and until Siff can switch him off, Li'l Mike. We work in three teams: Charlies to get us through the river into deep forest, Junior Rangers to guard the banks, and Delta Rangers to climb from the lower level and explore the mid-level.

Mission goals include finding native food, fuel, and a place to plant crops. The first two I'm confident of finding. Farmland is harder. The entire island is claimed by trees. Maybe we can hack out a place from old dead trunks in the mid-level. With solar powered light bulbs colonists could grow a farm in a cave in the island's interior.

We gather in an open port of the Homestead a short jump above the water. The river flows swiftly from the forest about five meters from the port. It'll be a struggle against the current so we bring a minimum of equipment. The Deltas have climbing gear, Juniors have kits with blasters, and the gill-breathing Charlies bring tow ropes to pull us through the water.

Surveys found small fish and eels testing edible and none that bite, but I fear what we'll find under tangled roots that arch over the river like the bulk of a mountain. No light can penetrate far through the dense vegetation so it will become black very quickly.

Ping waits for us down below until the Deltas arrive with climbing equipment packed into bags. Charlies are first into the water with cables for the rest of us to hang on to. Deltas follow and then the Junior Rangers, dropping two meters to splash into silted river water. Crystal is close to the edge, but she codes, [Thuy, carry me to the water. I'm wearing pumps.]

I step behind to lift her by the waist. "Ugh, how much do you weigh?"

[Quiet, you beast! I do have feelings you know.]

"Sorry, mon," I say in a low Jamaican accent.

[I'm heavier than normal. My arms have motorized pulleys and two hundred meters of steel cable.] Her hands are vicious looking pincers.

[But we're staying on the banks.]

[Unless we have to rescue the Deltas. Are you going to climb hand over hand?]

At the edge I set Crystal down and tip her over. With all the gear she sinks straight down out of sight. [Crystal!]

Her face reappears, hydrox mouthpiece in place. [I got the pumps on. Throw me my kit.]

I obey and hop into the water with my blaster and kit under one arm. With the other hand I grab a hook on the tow cable as the current threatens to sweep me into the bay. Swift and cold, the water seeps down from the forest canopy into the dark, last touching sunlight many days or weeks ago as rain.

In two lines we head into the forest. Anacine and Crystal pull Siff and I. Ping and the other two Charlies pull the two Delta Rangers. Like Crystal, Li'l Mike has water pumps in his legs. The Homestead drifts out of sight, as we duck under tangled roots trailing into the surface. Anacine codes to our line, [We're going down to hug the bottom. Slower water and fewer roots.]

Siff says, [I hope it's warmer.]

I agree, but a Delta can't admit to discomfort. I wonder if it gets cold enough whether my leech will release a little Gravitol. When the last sunlight is gone we swim by flashlight. White sand, torn leaves, and small glowing fish swirl around our heads as Charlies drag us forward. Roots hang in tangled clumps and slow our progress. They grasp at our packs. Anytime one of us hangs up it stops the whole line. We abandon the towline when the water slows enough to push and pull ourselves by the roots.

Each Ranger is assigned one Charlie to shepherd us up the river except for me. I get Crystal who powers us forward with water pumps for legs. Sharp steel hands pinch at my legs and feet whenever she thinks I'm going too slow. [Get along li'l doggie.]

[I'm warning you for the last time, Crystal! Why don't you go ahead of me and pull?]

[We're almost there. The others found an eddy pool. They're waiting for us before the ascent.]

We reach a side branch of the river, and as we float to the surface, sparks glow in vegetation over our heads. [Crystal, turn off your light.]

Soft blue spots appear along the wood like mushrooms. Crystal says, [Bioluminescent roots?]

[Animals most likely.]

As one of the lights slides along overhead, I turn my lamp back on. In the glare there's only a shape that looks like another branching root. [This place gives me the creeps, or as Lao Tsu would say, "Do not fight on a field of the enemies choosing."]

[Hang on to your nunchucks, it's just around the next turn.]

We sink and push along bedrock, curving around a family of roots as big as a house. We enter a clearing, with a natural dome of twisted roots overhead where Rangers have set up perimeter lights. Crystal takes off her mask, wrinkling her nose. "It smells like my Uncle Scooter, walks barefoot on country roads and never washes his feet."

We stand in freezing water to our waists while Thor and Rocky unpack climbing gear. Still wearing the hydrox mouthpiece Siff holds his blaster. Scanning root balls over our heads, Siff codes, [I feel like we're inside some alien's stomach.]

I take out my mouthpiece and wade over. "Mighty cold stomach acid. Where are the Deltas going to climb?"

There are breaks in the roots overhead ringed with oozing mud. Water drips everywhere. Delta Top says, "Rocky, up the hole!"

Stripped to a pair of shorts, Rocky ties a nylon rope around his waist. With a toothy grin he looks like a ghoul in our perimeter lights. He squeezes through a hole in the ceiling, and spiked boots bite into the roots with a chunk, chunk, chunk.

Thor growls, "The rest of you look sharp. Serena, ready the pulley motors. Juniors, you better look busy if you know what's good for you."

Blasters at the ready, Siff, Crystal, and I search every nook inside the root cave while Anacine and Terra duck back underwater to wait. Siff nods to the hole overhead. [Li'l Mike, why don't you follow Rocky.]

Sitting on a root, the mech sneers, "I got my orders."

Siff looks at me. [What does that mean?]

As we go round the empty cave, Rocky reports his progress from our watches, "I'm up twenty meters and it's still a maze of roots and mud. No clear shaft for the pulleys. We'll be climbing all the way."

"Signs of life?"

"Lizards, mud eels, squirrels: they're attracted to my lights."

"Try turning them off."

"No thanks."

After Junior Rangers tire of looking busy we find a relatively dry shelf of roots to sit. Crystal waves her steel claw hand. "Looks like I brought this along for nothing, mon." Crystal aims at a trunk on the other side of the dome. The hand explodes, flying across the cave and trailing a steel cable to thunk into a mass of roots. She flops the loose cable up and down, "It's on a spool." The cable pulls tight. "I was planning to ride cable up to the mid-level."

I say. "Sweet. Use the unorthodox to wage war."

And then the forest comes crashing in. Two heavy masses fall like logs through muddy holes in the ceiling. Thrashing in the water, they slice air with what we recognize immediately as mouths full of deadly teeth. Crystal's claw hand is incapacitated on the far side of the dome. The Charlies might be underwater with those beasts. Thor is against the wall, knife out and looking for a place to plunge. Siff and I sit on the roots in a daze, our blasters on our laps. I move first, raising the barrel towards the nearest of the slimy albino alligators. Thor yells, "Wait!" [Charlies, location?]

Charlie Top reports, [Searching branches off the river. What's your situation?]

[Unfriendlies in the cave. They dropped from holes in the ceiling. Watch your heads.]

One of the beasts snags a tooth on Crystal's cable, jerking her into the water. Delta Top yells at me, "What are you waiting for!"

My barrel has never stopped tracking. With Crystal in the water I choose bullets over explosives, firing three quick shots into each. The thrashing stops; waves of foul swamp water splash the walls, and dead albino alligators lay still on top. Thor growls, "Siff, check 'em for food." In the jawbone radio, he says, [Rocky, you hear?]

[Yeah, boss.]

[Return to camp and watch out for reptiles.]

[Are we aborting?]

[Small mission deserves small risk. We'll get to the mid-level another way.]

Delta Top has a disappointed look that shames me as Junior Rangers help Crystal chop her claw out of the root. We were on watch. Crystal codes, [We should have guessed this cozy little nest was someone's home.]

Siff codes, [So now we know. The meat's good too. What would his Highness Thor say if we lit a barbecue in here?]

I code, [Don't, Siff, he's right to be mad. In serving, do one's best. When being served, be gracious.]

Crystal says, "Where's Li'l Mike?"

The empty root where he was sitting is empty. Siff gets a hopeful look in his eye until the mech says, "Up here." We follow the voice to find Li'l Mike clinging upside down on a root overhead. He must have jumped when the fighting started.

Twenty minutes later Rocky slips through the same hole the alligators used. Thor looks over at us; our blasters lean against a far wall. He shakes his head. "New plan, Rangers. The forest sits on granite. We're going to make our own farmland.

We'll blast trees back five hundred meters to either side of the river."

Siff says, [Do you know how many billions of kilograms of wood you're going to have to move?]

Thor doesn't even answer. In his eyes we're now a security risk. I guess we were lucky with the alligators. A Ranger named Dave used to call me Pachinko after the game where silver marbles bounce down through a maze of pins and pockets.

As wave after wave of Junior Rangers got picked off, I kept bouncing with the luck of a pachinko ball. I even outlasted Dave. I'd like to think skill has as much to do with my continued survival but who can tell? Maybe luck is the payoff for hard work and vigilance.

Engines light once again to float the Homestead away from the carnage that is about to be loosened along the river. High explosives will crack trees loose from their roots. Hopefully they'll fall outwards into the bay like toppling grain silos.

The planet has everything colonists could want in abundance, but they would like to see open farmland along the banks and green shoots of Earth crops. We'll try to give them that before we leave.

Anacine and Li'l Mike stay in the bay with Ping. As trees fall, Charlie Rangers help drag them out of the way with the Black Widow. The other Junior Rangers are assigned to break into the mid-level forest, exactly what we started earlier. In our absence Ivan expanded the tunnel, and the Dragonfly chews its way deeper into the canopy.

Crystal sits in the copilot seat next to Ivan. Siff and I sit outside on the skids to warn Ivan if we drift. It's a dangerous strategy, but if our rotor gets damaged, at least the Dragonfly will be caught by interlocked branches. We wouldn't fall too far.

Siff and I have blasters to assist the Dragonfly's fifty caliber front teeth as Ivan flies us slowly along a tunnel twice the length of the Dragonfly. My blaster points to outcropping branches, and I'm careful to shoot far from the spinning rotor. It would be embarrassing to take out our own ship.

With Siff firing into the trees, I code, [Watch for ricochets into the blades. Try switching to burn.]

I set my blaster to shoot fire at an already damaged branch dangling by a strip of bark. The spout of flame washes over it, curling the leaves, but the branch hangs on stubbornly. I try a longer burst and then code Siff, [I can't burn these suckers. The leaves turn brown but even small sticks are flame resistant.]

[Back to bullets.]

I code to Crystal, [Has Bravo team checked this endless energy source for flammability yet?]

[Green wood ignites at eight hundred degrees.]

[That's hot enough to melt aluminum!]

[They're hoping that deadwood in the mid-level is easier to burn.]

Ivan says, [We're passing last of leaves. It's just trunks now. Get cable ready and you can dive in.]

The Dragonfly hovers inside the tunnel, heavy branches only a meter from rotor tips. As we put on harnesses, Ivan walks back to the hold to stretch. "Comrades, that was work!"

Siff says, [Shouldn't you be flying?]

"Is on auto-pilot. Holding one position, Dragonfly is more precise than I could ever be."

[You could watch the fuel gauge or something.]

"Stack register would warn me. I'm thinking of going out with you."

Crystal removes her legs. "Come on, mon. Tell 'em you're joking."

"Pilots never get fun of exploring."

As I pull on pieces of body armor, Ivan says, "Are you wearing full skids out there? You'll be too heavy to climb!"

I can feel myself turning red. Rocky climbed through the mud hole with only shorts and a knife. Siff says, [Leave him alone, Ivan.]

Even Siff doesn't wear armor but I can't take it off now. I would appear a puppet as well as a coward. I say to Ivan, "Why don't you make yourself useful and operate the crane?"

Ivan laughs but he walks over to ready the hook. Crystal goes first, still wearing pincher hands and pulley cable arms. They've been modified with stops so the claws don't bite so deep. She has no legs, choosing instead simple grabbers like the claws of birds. She looks like a nightmare metal midget but Ivan doesn't make jokes about her.

Crystal climbs out and grabs the hook. The cable drops her into the dark until Crystal codes, [Hold. Okay, I'm on a sturdy branch. Send the Tweedle brothers.]

Siff waves a hand, shouting over the roar of the Dragonfly's rotor, "You firtht, Dee."

"After you, Dum."

"No, no, I inthitht."

Siff really bugs me sometimes. I snatch the hook and ride it down to a horizontal branch as thick as a telephone pole. Crystal holds out a claw that I ignore as I step out on the branch. It's as dense and solid as rock. It's hard to believe the tree extends down to the ground another seven hundred meters!

Crystal perches on the branch next to me as we wait for Siff. Although not the pitch black of the swamp, it's dark enough to turn on area lights. Our kits cast spheres of shadows into a tangle of branching trunks. If there were natural light here there would also be leaves to gather it.

Life grows as a response to available energy, soaking it into high-energy chemical bonds. Ivan's voice comes from our watch speakers, "I'm going back to Homestead to save fuel. I won't be more than fifteen minutes away."

Crystal says, "Pick us up for lunch."

"Da, and don't do anything stupid."

"Right, mon." Crystal shoots her hand at a distant trunk. She jerks it once and swings across the dark gap.

Siff says, [Crystal, we're effectively on the top of a two-hundred story building.]

"We couldn't bounce more than five or ten stories before landing spread eagle on something."

[Can't argue with that.] Siff skips along our branch and launches himself over a three-meter gap. [I *love* low gee planets!]

I can't follow as fast in skids. Walking soberly along the branch, I start the work we were assigned. Finding fruits the size of apples and larger ones the size of cantaloupes, I code to Siff, [Alpha Ranger, get your gut over here.]

Circles of light surrounding Siff and Crystal bounce merrily through the forest like pixies. As Crystal gains confidence with her hands, she swings from branch to branch in perilous arcs. I can't be sure but I think Siff turns somersaults in the air. [Siff, get over here!]

[Whoa!]

Crystal codes, [What you got, mon?]

[I'm not sure.]

Crystal's sphere of light rises like an elevator until she reaches Siff. When the spheres of light merge, Crystal codes, [Whoa!]

I say, [Come on guys, stop joking.]

The others are a hundred meters away and slightly above, close to where the Dragonfly cut its way through the canopy. Following a maze of branches, I walk, climb, and backtrack before reaching the two standing at the edge of a wooden platform the size of a basketball court.

Dipping in the middle like a dinner plate, the platform's surface is rough but appears to be made from one giant horizontal branch smoothed with a rolling pin. Crystal shoots a claw into an overhead branch, swinging to the far rim.

Siff says, [Is it natural?]

I try to find a seam with my knife. "The wood must have been treated."

[With what?]

Crystal says, "By whom?"

Siff and I walk gingerly across the open platform, expecting at any moment to fall through a trapdoor in the wood. We hold kits more tightly, shining flashlights into the dark forest around us. I say, "We're down three hundred meters from the canopy. If this is a sun deck, the builders didn't plan too well."

Crystal says, "The forest grows skyward. At one time this spot was on top."

"You think there are newer platforms higher up?"

Siff says, [If there are, maybe they're occupied.]

Crystal shoots a claw to a branch overhead, rising on the cable.

I say, "Stick together; someone made this. Crystal, drop a rope."

We climb past small nets in the trees, some with fruit and some with lizard birds trapped inside. Siff examines the nets. [The material may be natural but they're tied with granny knots. Definitely manufactured. Thuy, are you sending video to the Homestead?]

"We're live. After he saw the platform, Lieutenant Nofree ordered us to stay out indefinitely. Delta will want to know who's trapping birds. That's a security issue."

Crystal drops back to our level, hanging from a cable like a yo-yo. "No platforms above but I've got an idea. I called Ivan back with the Dragonfly. We'll make camp out here."

"Where's he going to land?"

"Isn't it obvious?"

While waiting on the platform we gather fruits and animals from the nets. Siff sets them in a line, animal and vegetable mixed in courses. He presses each to an electronic gut, standard equipment for Alpha Rangers. If the gut says they're non-toxic, I try a bite directly from the plants. For animals I roast them first with my blaster. Non-toxic animals can still carry toxic bacteria.

My ancestors ate raw bush meat, but I'm softer and have a leech to protect me if poison gets through. Still, it can be a nasty business. The fruits are sour like old lemons dipped in battery acid. The lizard-birds are better, kind of like chicken. Most proteins have a similar bland taste on whatever world they're produced.

After Ivan arrives, we climb higher while the Dragonfly cuts through the last of mid-level forest. Bullets, sticks, and fruit rain down below. Ivan breaks through the last branches to settle the Dragonfly down gently. The platform barely moves but Ivan keeps the rotor going half-speed until he's sure it won't collapse.

He finally cuts the engine and steps out to join us for lunch. Shaking his head Ivan says, "Nice of world to provide helipad."

Crystal says, "Or not so nice. It may be a trap."

"At least it's quiet. You should hear racket back at Homestead, like three nuclear wars, and we can barely make dent on beach. Colonists may have to rethink farming."

Siff says, [There's plenty of good food in the forest, right Thuy?]

"So the gut says. Colonists can cook it with baking soda to neutralize the acidity."

From among the wood chips, bullet casings, and torn leaves scattered across the platform, Ivan picks up a tan object about ten-centimeters long. Carved from a piece of wood, it looks like a little canoe. "Who's into folk crafts?"

Crystal takes it in her claws. "It's a little boat, mon. Maybe people on Klondike-2 are five-centimeters tall."

Ivan says, "If they are, it would have taken years to haul boat up here from beach."

"Give me that," Siff snarls. [It's obviously a toy.]

I say, "Never use the word obvious on a colony planet. This is excellent construction. I bet it would float. Even if it's not meant to be used, it tells us the builder is familiar with water transport. Their territory must range from the sea to the treetops."

Ivan says, "Maybe they build large boats and paddle from island to island like Polynesians."

Crystal says, "And then climb up here to build a temple platform for their god."

"Enough speculation, colonists need facts. I could care less if five-centimeter Polynesians build temples. Our colonists need food, water, and energy. If mission succeeds, colonists will reconstruct planet history long after we're gone."

Siff hands the boat back. [I miss playing with toys. I had a marble collection that filled a bucket: steelies, puries, cateyes, bumblebees. I gave them to a friend before we left for the moon.]

Crystal says, "I used to have tea parties with my stuffed animals. I gave them to my little cousins."

As we talk about our favorite toys, Ivan takes the boat and stalks back to the Dragonfly. You would think his heart is hard as diamond, but at night I find him playing with the boat in the kitchen sink. "Is hydrodynamic experiment," he growls.

When I first saw Klondike-2's lush forests I thought we struck gold. Right now it looks more like gold-painted tin with peeling flakes. A normal forest provides fuel and soil. Klondike-2 wood is too dense to burn. Trees block available land with tons of tangled, matted trunks. While colonists try to rip out some of that vegetation with high explosives, Junior Rangers have an easier time.

The Dragonfly rests securely on a wood terrace high in the trees. We're free to explore the mid-level. No sunlight penetrates the canopy high above but we're bathed in the warm outside lights of the Dragonfly. Sitting on rough wood around a lunch of sbeef hot dogs, chips, potato salad, and cold drinks, Crystal ticks points on her claws, "One, we have to find out who made this platform, two, are there any more like it, and three, what are they for?"

Siff raises a finger. [And four, can we find some way to get Anacine out of dragging logs across the bay?]

"If Anacine comes back, we get Li'l Mike as well."

I say, "Why'd he go with her in the first place? I thought Li'l Mike wanted to show off his climbing ability?"

"Maybe the gators changed his mind."

We share a laugh, and I look around the dark forest. "No water up here. No need for Charlie Rangers."

"But the canoe…"

A concussive boom echoes off trunks around us. Siff says, [The Homestead?]

Ivan taps his pogs for data. "Thunderstorm up top."

I hold out a hand for raindrops. "No water."

When we're pulsed by another thunderclap, Crystal says, "Sounds like mean lightning. I'm glad the forest *doesn't* burn so easily. Maybe lightning storms forced Klondike-2 trees to grow tough."

I say, "And maybe that's how the forest can grow so tall. Tough trees have never been cleared by fire."

Siff looks at my Klondike melon. [You going to finish that?]

"Help yourself."

[Not for me. If lunch is over we should go exploring.] Siff heaves the melon over the side listening for a splatter below.

"That's littering. In another million years someone might slip on that goop."

[The ants will get it.]

Ivan says, "Okay comrades, let's find out how terrace formed. Crystal and I will take far side."

As Crystal swings away on a cable arm, Ivan follows more slowly on boots. With flashlights shining and fingers on blaster triggers, Siff and I walk towards our side. The terrace is wide but dips in the middle. It's not made of a single bough like I first thought. Climbing down and looking underneath, boughs from different trees twist round and about, fusing into the structure of the platform.

I run my hand across the top looking for a seam, "It's like they melted together."

Siff says, [Could it be natural?]

"I didn't think so but now I'm not so sure."

A drop of water hits the back of my neck. Over the next several minutes a steady drip-drip-drip sounds all around us. [The rain is finally here. Maybe we should wait it out in the Dragonfly.]

Crystal codes to us, [Junior Rangers, you find anything?]

Siff codes, [The terrace is made of a bunch of trunks all fused together like a raft. How about you?]

[The trees aren't as solid as we thought. Some of the trunks are hollow.]

Ivan codes, [Get over here, Thuy. We need your skinny bones to climb down inside one of holes.]

Ivan and Crystal stand at the edge of the platform next to a trunk two meters in diameter. The tree rises straight up overhead and down below out of the sight of Ivan's flashlight. Ivan says, "Looks like some sort of load bearing column, not so twisted like others."

Under increasing drips, Siff says, [Where's the hole?]

Crystal says, "Over here."

Perched on the far side of the trunk, Crystal shines her flashlight on an opening. On hands and knees I stick my head in. Within the flashlight's beam, a shaft extends both up and down. Ivan says, "You going in?"

"I'm too wide."

"Not if you strip off skids."

I don't like the way Siff and Crystal look at me. "Maybe after the rain. The shaft may be some kind of water transport system."

Siff backs me, [He won't be able to see his feet. An alligator could come up.]

Ivan pauses and then nods. "We still have to find out if terrace is unique."

Crystal says, "We already searched skyward. We can go down and stay ahead of the rain."

Siff says, [With a pulley and elevator off the platform we could drop down through the mid-level.]

As we secure a pulley to the tough wood, we see firsthand how dense it is. Even with Crystal's hydraulic driver the screw only goes in halfway. Ivan rattles the hardware. "That'll hold."

Crystal says, "If a lot of these trees are hollow it may explain how the forest can grow so high. The trunks are light and strong."

We're seven hundred meters above the forest floor. There's no direct path down so we lower ourselves with the pulley, place another box, and lower again. The rain follows us down making the footing slippery and soaking our clothes.

Attracted to the light, lizard-birds fly out of the dark, flashing by our heads, and we sense bigger creatures beyond our sight. They don't make a sound nor do they approach. In the glimpses of a flashlight, Siff and Crystal's camera eyes identify dark blue. Fortunately, not the white of alligators.

After an hour we take a break on our endless descent into the dark. Siff stretches out on a bough when a melon slams into the wood centimeters from his head. Siff squeaks and almost goes over the side, until Crystal catches him. "He's bleeding!" Crystal holds Siff's shoulders with her claws.

Red goop plasters Siff's head and torso. He wipes his eyes and gently probes his skull. [No, no, it's okay. Melon pulp, not brain pulp.]

I say, "It's karma for that melon you threw over."

Siff cleans up with water from his kit. [You think someone threw this?]

"I didn't say that. Ripe melons must fall all the time."

Siff rubs his eyes. [It burns.]

"You should try eating one."

Ivan examines a shattered piece of rind and tosses it over. "No harm done. Shall we continue down?"

Siff looks up into the dark. [Maybe we should try again tomorrow. If this *was* an attack, we're getting further from the ship.]

Crystal says, "And don't forget those alligators below."

[Exactly!]

I say, "She's joking, Siff. Danger is our business."

[Easy for you to say wrapped in skids.]

Siff's still shaken by the near miss. He doesn't mean it but the words sting. A minute later he says, [Sorry, Thuy. With or without skids, you're the toughest Ranger I know.]

I bow and ready the pulley for our next drop.

Halfway between canopy and swamp, we find another terrace. About a third the size of the first, it appears ancient. Seams between flattened boughs give the platform a warped parquet. There's another hollow trunk near one side. Rainwater running from the hole collects in a pool in the shallow depression of the platform. I say, "See? Water flows through the trunks. I might have drowned."

After a quick inspection we gather near the edge of the pool to discuss our options. Crystal says, "Pretty exciting, mon. Should we spend the night here and continue down in the morning?"

Ivan nods. "These platforms are definitely artifacts. and pool of water adds to significance. Maybe they're reservoirs."

Siff says, [We can bring Anacine out to look at the hollow trees.]

"Already done. I coded Charlie Top. We pick up Anacine tomorrow."

I say, "And would the First Engineer be coming along as well?"

"I'm sure Terra has better things to do."

As we stand on the platform talking, Junior Rangers can't help but smile. We'll all be together again and on a relatively safe adventure, several mysteries yet to solve. It doesn't get better than this.

Crystal yawns, "I'm beat. Even with machine arms I don't think I could climb back up."

Siff says, [Ivan, did you lock the Dragonfly?]

"I'm telling her to lock up now. We should set alarms around platform as well. Thuy, I assume you brought heat and motion sensors?"

"Of course. Come on, Siff, we'll set up layers in concentric spheres. Do we want to wake with every squirrel, lizard, or ant?"

Siff says, [We'll be in sleeping bags. Bigger than a bunny will be safe.]

"The fluffy killer test."

Siff and I set motion alarms in branches around the platform. When we get back, Crystal and Ivan have set up lights to cast a warm glow on our forest terrace. Crystal nods to the pool. "Care for a dip before bedtime? I'm sweaty as a horse."

Siff says, [Is the water clean?]

"Condensed rainwater, no atmospheric pollutants."

[pH?]

"Slightly acidic, but don't worry about me. I'll take prosthetics off." With metallic clicks, Crystal's arms and feet-claws detach, falling into a pile. A helpless torso lying on the wood, she says, "Little help?"

As Ivan scoops her up and walks towards the pool, she says, "Face up, please."

We sit in the water letting tension drain from our muscles. It's impossible to fully relax on a new planet. With so many unknowns the slightest mistake can be fatal, but Klondike-2 is as close to a National Park as I've seen. I still don't trust to luck, wearing body armor even to bathe. With hard work and vigilance, little Pachinko will survive another world.

The water is deep enough to take a few strokes. I roll facedown, dog-paddling away from the others when my fingers brush across a loose stone at the bottom. I stop and feel around in the dark finding three of the stones tucked into a groove of the platform. I bring them back to the light, astonished to find three almost perfectly spherical stones colored red, blue, and gray.

When I hold them up to the others, Siff's mouth drops open. [Marbles. Where did you find them?]

"Along the floor. You really think they're marbles?"

Siff takes the gray one. [Chipped. They're marbles all right.]

Crystal says, "I guess our platform builders got thumbs to shoot."

I say, "So platforms are playing courts for marbles?"

"Marbles are for kids. Platforms are places where families gather. Can't have a family reunion stretched out along a branch."

Ivan nods. "You may want to reconsider security arrangements, Thuy."

"What do you mean? We put out motion sensors."

"Intelligent species might find way around sensors. We haven't seen them, and we're in their territory. We need all of warning we can get if they attack."

"I'm not going to stay awake all night just because we found a few marbles. My instincts tell me that motion sensors will suffice."

"I think electronic gadgets replaced your instincts. When I first joined Junior Rangers, I heard stories. You were legend, but I don't think that old Thuy would even recognize you now."

"Stay up if you want. Hackman and I will sleep just fine."

Near the water in the middle of the platform we unroll sleeping bags and insect netting. After I turn off perimeter lights, faint sparks appear in the forest around us. Tucked in so far from the sun, mid-level animals produce their own bioluminescent light. That takes energy. I wonder where they get it from so far from the sun? Must be from eating fruit fallen from the canopy.

Episode 4 – Two Farms

We wake to our watch alarms, buried deep in mid-level. The morning sunlight last touched these trunks a hundred thousand years ago. I turn on my kit globe to pack for the long climb back to the Dragonfly. We'll ride motorized pulleys but there's a lot of stooping, kicking, and stretching to get around branches. When I crawl out of a warm bag into freezing air, Siff is already packed and blowing on his hands.

I stretch my back. "I don't care how thick the air cushion, my spine knows I'm not in my own cot."

Ivan snorts and sips hot coffee. "Delta Ranger faces hardship on alien world."

"I got the same equipment you do."

"I don't pretend I'm survivor."

Siff says, [Give it a rest, Ivan. Would you be happy if Thuy slept naked on a branch last night?]

"If he had we might not have been robbed."

I look at Crystal but she gives no hint. "The perimeter lights!"

Ivan smirks. "They're gone, and robber tried to unscrew pulley. Fortunately, they failed. I'm afraid of what we might find further up. If we have to climb trunks by hand it will take all day."

I put on pogs to check data from the alarms. "Nothing bigger than a bunny got within a twenty meters of this platform."

"Then some amazingly strong bunnies dragged off our lights."

Siff says, [Maybe they moved behind the trees.]

"No," I say stubbornly. "The lines of sight are clear."

Crystal says, "Glad I kept my prosthetics inside the bag."

I feel the statement as an accusation. As part of Delta, I'm responsible for security. "I'll set traps tonight. The perimeter lights may be gone, but I can leave my flashlight as bait. The thieves are probably the builders of these platforms. That information is worth the loss of a few lights."

Ivan says, "Although you rationalize, that *would* be consolation prize. Let's get Anacine and make plans."

Crystal uses a circular handsaw to cut a sample of platform wood for the lab. "Maybe the treated wood will burn easier. Bravo First thinks we may have to look for a more attractive fuel source like dried seaweed."

Ivan says, "And Anacine will go back with Charlies to collect seaweed. Absence makes heart grow fonder, eh Siff?"

[It does cut down on the fights.]

Crystal leads the way up. If our pulleys have been tampered with she can catch a fall with web-slinging cable arms. Ivan follows Crystal, then Siff, and then me. I hook my belt clamp onto the cable and use my jawbone radio to tell the pulley above to reel me in. I kick to clear branches, and keep my blaster pointing into the dark. I can slow or speed the motor depending on the density of vegetation around me. When I reach the top of a lift, Siff is just disappearing into the sky. We're strung out over two hundred vertical meters of forest.

On the sixth lift, the others are waiting on a branch. "Don't tell me the pulley's gone."

Siff says, [This is where I nearly bought it.]

"Bought what?"

He points to a depression in the wood. [The falling melon... karma.]

It looks like the melon left a dent in the branch. "The fruit did that?"

Siff rubs his head gingerly. Ivan says, "After melon shattered I don't remember hole like that."

Crystal says, "Definitely not, mon. It was juice and rind, something Uncle Scooter would leave behind." She saws a piece of dented wood for the lab before we start up again.

I don't disconnect the pulleys and cables behind me; we plan to return to the lower platform later today. Hopefully I can get our lights back and catch the thieves. I hate being ripped off.

The storm that filled the pool on the lower platform also left standing water on the upper platform. The water's not as deep, but it will take weeks to evaporate. It's a nice little reservoir for any nomadic tribe of tree-dwellers. We board the Dragonfly and Ivan backs us out of the tunnel into harsh sunlight. As we turn and head parallel to the coast, our entrance into the forest is rapidly lost from sight. I wonder how Ivan finds it again, pilot instinct or the satellite positioning system?

Flying along the coast it takes only minutes to get back. The picturesque bay we left has been turned into a logging town. Explosions shake the forest, filling the river outflow with torn leaves and mud. Earthmovers crawl the riverbanks trying to clear logjams while tons of water builds in the trees behind. Motorized boats pull rafts of sticks and logs across the bay, parking them along the banks or shoving them into the ocean.

For all the effort, there is little evidence of progress. The forest is too massive, too many Gigagrams of wood rising above each square meter of land. Ivan says, "You have to admire determination."

I quote Lao Tsu, "Small amounts are obtainable, large amounts confusing."

"They could farm fish, become an ocean colony instead of land."

"Only as last resort. People like dirt under feet, and worms between toes."

Siff says, [I wonder what's happening on Polyhyd-4. When we left, every colonist was getting gills. How desperate we are to leave Earth.]

"Polyhyd-4 wasn't that bad. They had methane vents for fuel gas, floating islands of vegetation to build homes, plenty of rainfall, sea animals and vegetables. If Anacine had been with us she might have defected."

Ivan says, "Was before my time as well. How many missions have you been on Thuy?"

"Too many," I say sadly, faces of old friends flashing through my mind.

When I was younger, I wasn't interested in Eastern philosophy, or any philosophy for that matter. I lived day-to-day, mission to mission, trusting reflexes to see me through. As fellow orphans fell to the sides, people looked at me differently. What did I have that those other unfortunates didn't? I couldn't offer reasons myself so I clammed up.

Silence was even worse. Rangers suspected me of having secrets that I was unwilling to share. Instead of offering weak excuses or none at all, I offered bits of wisdom. Cobbled together from many sources, they are in no way helpful to giver or receiver. It did shut people up though.

I believe in the power of nature and the prudence of adapting one's actions to her will. I don't believe the universe operates with unseen purpose. Let others take what they will from my collections of sayings. They would be far better served by that old chestnut, look before you leap.

Crystal says, "Someday we'll find an unlimited source of power. We'll go back and visit all those colony worlds we helped seed."

Siff says, [That's what Anacine wants. Go back to the best world to settle down and raise a family.]

Ivan says, "After life of Ranger she would be bored out of mind."

Crystal says, "Just because you're not risking your neck every minute doesn't mean boring. I grew up in a small house on a quiet, tree-lined street. I remember a lot of home cooked meals, laughter, games, and loving parents. I remember nothing of boredom."

The talk of family hits all of us orphans hard. We're quiet on the return trip. As the Dragonfly settles onto the back of the Homestead we hear rumors of a radical plan. Explosives are knocking down trees but there's too much residue. Engineers will use the Homestead's engines to clear an area with a controlled burn. It won't matter how dense the wood is. The Homestead's backwash will split atoms into plasma.

Ivan parks the Dragonfly and we work our way down through the Homestead. We pack a lunch at the cafeteria and meet Anacine, Li'l Mike, and Ping at sea level. With feet dangling in the water we eat and watch the forest from across the bay. Crystal has on normal arms and legs again between assignments. "Looks like the work is slowing down."

Anacine says, "As of half an hour ago Charlie Rangers are off transportation detail. We're making a survey of the bay to see what might happen if we blast a square kilometer patch of forest."

"Around the river mouth?"

"We still need fresh water."

I say, "It'll be a disaster. Talk about annoying Mother Nature. There's a whole ecosystem in there we don't know anything about. The canopy catches rain that filters down through mid-level into a complex swamp. If you clear the forest to bedrock you'll see flooding like you wouldn't believe."

"Until a new equilibrium is established. We won't be around to see how that turns out."

Siff says, [There must be a better way.]

Anacine says, "The water's perfect. Colonists could get gills and live free like Ping and I."

[How about light bulbs to grow plants in the swamp?]

"Alligators."

Crystal says, "And colonists still don't have energy to power those lights. No fuel for generators. Solar panels in the treetops would be vulnerable to storms, and shake loose as branches bend in the winds."

"They could put solar panels on rafts. I'm telling you, mates, the trees are bad news."

The mech's head spins towards each speaker. Unlike previous missions it doesn't comment or ask questions. Li'l Mike seems preoccupied. I say, "Li'l Mike, any thoughts?"

I feel a chill when the mech gives me an appraising stare. "We should go on a long hike in the forest."

"Why's that?"

"I'm sure we'll find what we're looking for."

We finish lunch while boats return to tie up at the Homestead. Earth-moving machines shake mud out of their shovels and line up in the shallow water of the beach. We've heard nothing official, but Ivan says, "I guess they decided they're going to melt those suckers down to roots."

I feel bad about hundred thousand year old trees. It's always better working within an existing ecosystem than trying to create a new one. Crystal says, "We should get out of here before they put us to work hauling mud."

Our watches all beep simultaneously. "Junior Rangers, this is Nofree. I have an assignment for you."

Siff looks at the mech, and coughs, "Thpy!"

Ivan thumbs the watch radio. "Sir?"

"We're able to burn both samples of wood that Crystal submitted to the lab. We'd like to get further samples and have the Junior Rangers take a census of the number of platforms available."

"Will do. Have you decided to burn forest?"

"Affirmative. To save fuel we'll unload the Homestead tonight, and burn back the forest tomorrow morning. Ivan, transport the Junior Rangers as necessary."

Ivan salutes his watch. "Your wish is command to me."

"Of course it is. Nofree out."

When the watch beeps for disconnect, Anacine says, "Sarcasm is wasted on the Rangers. They know we wouldn't dare show disrespect."

Crystal points at Li'l Mike. "Sssttt!"

"You got a short circuit, mate?"

I say wisely, "A man without blame doesn't mind a glass house. For the guilty man, even stone walls are not enough." That shuts 'em up.

We still have hours of daylight. Colonists will use all of these and keep working through the night unloading the Homestead. Every drop of fuel is precious. There's no more coming from Earth, and Klondike-2's unimpressive geology isn't likely to produce oil.

The Junior Ranger's assignment isn't so straightforward. We're supposed to count the number of platforms buried inside a forest two-kilometers tall. The two we found already were a hundred meters and five hundred meters below the canopy. We have no idea how to find others.

Ivan flies close to the forest, hoping the Dragonfly's rotors will part the leaves to let us see in. "I'm setting radar to scan for echoes bouncing off flat surfaces."

Crystal says, "You're going to get false positives off the big trees."

"That's why Junior Rangers will have to go in for look. Prepare hoist, you can take turns on hook."

Siff says, [Why should *we* go down? We got the perfect anchor in Li'l Mike here.]

"He doesn't know what to look for."

The mech stares out the window long moments. "I'm an interactive learner. If you take me down into the trees, I can see what you're looking for."

[Thanks anyway, Li'l Mike. Maybe next time.]

I take the first turn, waiting on the skid with body armor and a belt around my waist. I don't care how much Ivan smirks. Hard work and vigilance are not empty philosophies. The Dragonfly slows to a hover, moving slowly over the canopy. Ivan says, "Got something solid a hundred meters down."

Siff says, [Dropping hook.]

As I enter freefall into the canopy, I yell through the jawbone, [Hey! It looks soft from up there. Down here it's all sticks.]

[Sorry, Thuy. You got the motor.]

[Thanks very much.] Through my jawbone radio I control cable speed as I kick down through a maze of branches. [I'm a hundred meters down. No platform, but there are some very large trunks.]

[Da, come on up.]

We keep flying. On the sixth drop, Anacine's second, she shrieks through the jawbone, [Crikey! It's the size of a basketball court. You've got to see this!]

[We're taking census, not sightseeing.]

Crystal says, [Come on, mon, I'm tired. I want to see it, and I may just find one of my old rag dolls.]

Anacine says, [You could almost fit the Dragonfly in here. I see you through the leaves. There are only a couple of big trunks in the way.]

[It wouldn't hurt to have second helipad in forest.]

I say, [What about the light poles? I thought we were going back to the lower platform tonight.]

Crystal says, [Forget 'em, Thuy. They're on the colony's budget. They won't care about a few light poles if we find something good.]

Li'l Mike helps us wrap explosives around thick trunks above the platform. As the mech scampers up and down trees with a pack of dynamite on his back, I realize how helpful a survival mech could be. Doc Blaitel's project has merit. Maybe we've been too hard on Li'l Mike; it can't be easy being the new teammate.

Embedded with razor wire, energy released from the explosions could cut through concrete. Even so, it takes a second round of explosives to carve a hole big enough for the Dragonfly to squeeze through and settle on the terrace platform. It's nearing nightfall; the sky dims in the jagged tear in canopy above our heads.

A million kilograms of wood slamming down through the forest should have wiped out all life around the platform. I still put out a few light poles and an overlapping alarm system of heat and motion sensors that an ant would trigger. I'll probably be up all night chasing down Klondike-2 ants but I won't be labeled incompetent.

We have dinner on the terrace but sleep in the Dragonfly. Alarms untouched, I sleep soundly and wake in my own bunk in the morning. Over breakfast Ivan says, "Homestead will be blasting forest soon. That should be spectacular sight."

Anacine points to our suspected spy in Li'l Mike. She winks broadly. "Lieutenant Nofree would want us to continue the platform census, not hang around like a bunch of tourists."

Crystal gives the okay signal with metal thumb and forefinger. "But Anacine, platforms near the bay would be most accessible for colonists. We could look for platforms as the trees come down."

I say, "And we could take a long break to watch the burn!"

Junior Rangers shake arms and heads. Ivan says, "Nyet, Thuy, no time. We only found three platforms. Colonists need more fuel than that."

"Ahh, so," I say, pointing to Li'l Mike. "Lieutenant Nofree will be happy with us for attending to duty."

Siff slaps his forehead. Of course I know what they're doing, but sometimes I like to play clueless. It amazes me they could believe I'm so stupid. Do I make it easy?

We put out the hook in case Lieutenant Nofree *is* watching and head back to the bay. The Dragonfly hovers inconspicuously over a beach two kilometers away while the Homestead rises against a green background of forest. As big as the Homestead is, she looks no match for the living mountain of vegetation.

There's no fuel to waste so the Homestead charges immediately, directing plasma exhaust at the ancient tangle of wood. We huddle behind Ivan's shoulders trying to get the best view as the Homestead falls, slowly carving slices out of the forest like a knife through cheese. We cheer as the wall of green is replaced by a strip of brown trunks growing above the gleaming white ship. Siff says, [They're through the canopy!]

On every drop the Homestead melts through a patch the size of a football field. As she gets closer to the swamp, huge clouds of steam billow out. The Homestead rises again from the cloud, repositioning for another pass. Anacine says, "They're leaving the swamp intact."

Ivan says, "Too much steam for air intakes. If Homestead's engines go out she'll join swamp permanently."

Crystal says, "I guess hand clearing a square kilometer of swamp is better than a cubic kilometer of wood."

I shake my head. "If they can even get in. With all that debris, the river will dam. To clutch at is to lose."

"What is the alternative?"

"Klondike natives live in trees. Why couldn't our colonists?"

"Eating fruit that tastes like battery acid?"

"Eating farm grown fruits and vegetables."

"There's no farmland, that's the problem."

"No farmland yet, but there *are* flat places to spread soil."

It takes hours for the Homestead to clear a square kilometer of forest above the swamp. It takes only seconds to convince Captain Wallen to let Junior Rangers set up an experimental farm on one of the treetop platforms. Ivan and Crystal will continue the count of platforms, while Siff, Anacine, Li'l Mike, and I try to set up a farm.

A quick calculation shows that our colonists could live comfortably in clans of twenty spread over a hundred platforms. Piece of cake. We already found three. If colonists are unable to clear the swamp, the platform farms will give them another option. That's what the Rangers are all about. I just hope the native platform-builders don't get upset when we try to move in.

We return to where we spent the night. With a couple of small missiles, Ivan clears out more of the shading branches, and lands the Dragonfly in a green bowl. Hot sunlight spills down inside. We still have to figure out a water supply for our farm, but we have a wide sunny space to work.

We open the hatch and walk around on the platform plotting strategy. There are still centimeters of water in the middle left over from the rain. Crystal says, "It rains enough here in the tropics we don't need a river. We just need a reservoir and sheets to catch the rain. Colonists could store water in bags stretched between the trunks."

Anacine says, "Maybe it's the rainy season right now. That may not last."

"The planet has only a small axial tilt. This will be about the same weather all year round."

"The sunlight's the same but wind and cloud patterns could change."

I say, "The trees are green. They're getting water from somewhere."

Anacine nods. "It can't be rising all the way from the swamp. Gravity pulls on liquids the same as solids, and electrostatic forces won't lift water a kilometer off the ground. Besides, these aren't even the same trees as the ones at the bottom. Colony scientists ran tests. Trees at the bottom are the great-great-great-grandparents of the trees on top. Offspring build on their parents below."

Siff says, [That melon that almost killed me could have been planting a seed.]

I say, "No wonder the melon tastes like acid. It eats its way through tough bark. So I guess we set up the farm now and worry about water later."

Crystal says, "We can set up sheets to catch rain. For thirsty crops we can set up a piping system down into the swamp."

Siff says, [We're going to need dirt up here, Ivan.]

"I'll drive truck. You work shovel."

I say wisely, "After a war, famine is bound to follow."

Siff says, "How ith that relevant?"

It's in bad taste to question an oracle. "Isn't it obvious," I say, heading for the open hatch of the Dragonfly. If Siff is going to try to find meaning, I'll have to be even more cryptic. I turn back. "When an advancing enemy crosses water, don't meet him at the water's edge. It's advantageous to allow half his force to cross and then strike."

We don't have far to look for dirt. The colony site is a square kilometer of smoking compost. There's probably more than a few white alligators baked into the goop. We shovel chunky black potting soil onto a tarp while all around us colony earthmovers scoop, pry, and push the mess into piles. It looks like an industrial dump.

The Dragonfly carries the tarp slung under her belly like dead prey as we head back over the forest. After the stinking mess is dropped onto the platform, Siff, Li'l Mike, and I stay to spread while Crystal and Anacine go back with Ivan for another load. Although it's a lot in weight, the soil doesn't spread very far. We'll be hauling several days if we want to cover the whole platform. For proof of concept we'll only plant a small patch.

Li'l Mike doesn't get tired, but Siff and I sweat in the humidity and heat. Taking a water break, Siff codes, [Don't look now but we're being watched.]

I casually take a drink of water while scanning the forest. [I count three.]

Li'l Mike says, [Nineteen.] The mech has camera eyes with wavelength discrimination.

I pull my blaster closer and click off the safety. [Set for burn. We'll get a wide spray and we don't have to worry about the trees lighting up.]

[They don't seem threatening.]

[We're spreading waste on their platform, of course they're threatening. These are the blue scaly things we saw below?]

[Blue scales, webbing from elbow to hip, possibly for gliding. Two large eyes centered on the top of a thin, egg-shaped head. Flexible neck like the body of a snake swivels the head in all directions.]

[Teeth?]

[On the side of the head, saber tooth style for puncture and killing.]

[They could be for scratching insects out of bark.]

[One could hope. They're obviously intelligent or they would have attacked already. Plus, they travel in social packs, and they probably built this platform which implies tool using.]

Li'l Mike says, [Should I scare them off?]

[Stay still. Rangers need to gather information, not react in panic.]

I say, [They probably tied the net traps. Definitely carnivorous.]

[You seem especially worried about being eaten.]

[I *am* security. What should we call these things? I see a few hanging from their tails. How about iguanas? Shall we see if they're edible?]

[As long as they don't attack, we should maintain peace in our adopted neighborhood. Besides, they make toys. It would be like killing Santa's elves.]

[Roger that. I would however like to return to that lower platform. If we can follow them back to their nest we may get our light poles back.]

Li'l Mike climbs slowly up a tree. [I'll circle round and keep watch.]

Siff says, [Get back here! You're going to provoke a fight,] but Li'l Mike is already through the leaves.

I code, [I wonder how many iguana tribes are in this forest?]

[For all the cubic meters available it could be thousands. Back to work?]

We sling blasters over our shoulders and pick up shovels to spread the mud. We work near the middle but iguana webbing is a concern. If the whole troop sails down on us at once it could get very bad very quick. At least they don't seem to be talking to each other, coordinating. While we work, iguanas maintain their vigil. Li'l Mike doesn't respond to our calls. If he's been taken, at least I have a jawbone recording warning him to stay.

In the hour it takes Ivan to return with another load, not one of the iguanas leaves as far as we can tell. When we hear the Dragonfly's rotor, Siff explains the situation. Ivan says, [You want me to scatter them with slugs?]

I say, [You might hit the mech. Besides, we're trying to avoid that scene. Just drop the soil and park the Dragonfly. I have a feeling iguanas are the builders of these platforms. They may have a lot to tell us.]

[They may be good eating.]

[Siff and I already had that conversation. Before we leave this planet, I promise we'll dine on iguana.]

We sit awhile in the Dragonfly observing the creatures through different lenses. They don't approach, so eventually we get out and spread the second load of soil. Crystal leans on her shovel. "Four square meters. Not much, but I guess we got enough to test."

Anacine says, "I'll bring out plants. You sterilize the soil."

I set my blaster for burn, and send a flaming red jet centimeters above the soil. As steam rises from the surface, iguanas fly out of the forest. I don't hear shouted warnings until I'm knocked sprawling. Ivan is inside the Dragonfly, Anacine has no blaster, and mine is in the mud.

Siff and Crystal take aim but don't fire as iguanas gallop across the platform like horses. Li'l Mike reappears, streaking out of the darkness to tackle one of the iguanas. About the same size they wrestle at the edge of the platform. Anacine shouts, "Li'l Mike, no!"

The iguana scrabbles frantically with all four legs. Li'l Mike's shirt is shredded as he fights to hold on. With an alien squeal the iguana makes ones last effort, jumping over the side into the trunks to disappear. Li'l Mike walks back, proudly holding out a section of tail that still twitches. "I got a sample."

I stand up in the mud with my knife. "Good job, Li'l Mike."

Ivan runs out with his blaster yelling at Siff, "Why didn't you shoot?"

[They weren't trying to hurt him.]

Anacine says, "It's the fire they were after. When it was gone they took off."

With the knife blade I wipe at a muddy cut along my forearm. "I'm glad you're able to show such great restraint. At least Li'l Mike did *something*."

Siff says, [We might have hit you. We're not Delta Rangers.]

"You're a better shot than that. You think these things are cute."

Ivan nods. "Shoot first, regrets later."

Crystal says, "What's that supposed to mean, mon?"

"We're paid to make hard decisions and live with consequences. How many worlds will you see if you can't bring yourself to counter threat? Look at Thuy. He's completely ruthless and he's survived longer than anyone."

"I wouldn't say ruthless," I say, wondering what they must think of me.

Anacine takes my arm. "That's bad. How do you feel?"

I'm surprised to see dripping blood. "I guess the Gravitol's kicking in."

"I should clean it. Come on into the Dragonfly."

Crystal says, "Come on, Li'l Mike. We'll analyze that iguana tissue as well. Where were you anyway?"

"Hiding in a hollow trunk."

"When they started moving why didn't you say something?"

The mech is quiet long moments, and then says, "I didn't know they were attacking."

Siff says, [More like you didn't know if the attack would be successful.]

I'm not as suspicious as Siff, but it does seem odd that Li'l Mike showed up so late in the action. We're more careful over the next few days. We keep blasters handy and forget about sterilizing the soil. Iguanas still gather in the shadows but they don't bother us as we tend our growing farm.

On the fifth day after landing, our third on the platform, skies darken and fill with clouds. By early afternoon a heavy rain falls through the jagged tear in the canopy, washing our crops away. "All our hard work," Anacine groans.

Ivan says, "Maybe we shouldn't have cleared out covering branches."

I say, "It wouldn't matter if we left the canopy in place. Water streams through the platform and pools in the middle."

Crystal says, "We should have built our farm along the sides. Rain runs across the deck from east to west. If we set up barricades we could still save the soil."

Anacine jumps up. "My gills are dry anyway."

Siff says, [I'll get a raincoat. Do we bring blasters?]

Ivan says, "I'll sit at door with mine. You can all go play in mud."

Crystal says, "Let me pop on some rubber limbs."

Our plants tilt in the downpour. If we have any soil left we can set the plants upright after the soil dries. Water washes across the deck tearing muddy streams along the edges. I code, [We need gutters along the sides.]

Crystal says, [How about cutting some tree branches? In this rain I'm sure the iguanas will stay home, wherever home is.]

Li'l Mike walks over from the Dragonfly. [I'll go out with you, Crystal, and stand guard.]

With her hand blade Crystal cuts branches, and Li'l Mike disappears into the trees to look for iguanas. We lay branches around the plot to staunch the flow of mud. By early evening the rain slows, and we sit outside the open hatch of the Dragonfly enjoying the contrast of warm air and cool rain. Even Ivan seems to relax. "Too bad we only have few more weeks."

Anacine says, "We've proven the feasibility of platform farming at least. We have soil, sunlight, and a reservoir of water. Colonists could even build shelves and grow their farms above terrace pools."

"I would like to show colonists nice even rows of plants."

I say, "We can set out heat lamps to dry the soil. The radiation will also jump start photosynthesis."

Ivan slaps feet in a puddle. "When rain stops. It's too nice of evening to work. I wish Li'l Mike had held on to that iguana. We could have had barbecue."

Siff says, [You don't even know what they taste like.]

"We could eat it charred or rolled in spices. There's nothing so delicious as hunting own meal. After couple years as Ranger, stem-cell meat doesn't challenge me anymore."

Anacine says, "You're all heart, Ivan. What if iguanas wanted to eat you?"

"I don't know that they don't."

We microwave prepackaged dinners inside the Dragonfly. Stem-cell pork and rice taste fine to me. Siff and I finish early and set heat lamps along soggy rows of soil. Siff says, [We can set the plants upright tomorrow.]

I walk back to sit with the others while Siff patches wires into the Dragonfly's generator. As red coils glow to life we shiver in a warming breeze of air. We lay back to watch stars over our little green bowl of paradise when I hear a security warning over my jawbone radio. The stack register announces, [Perimeter breach, north and west, two targets, each masses over thirty kilos, three targets, four, five, six, seven...]

"Iguanas coming in fast," I yell, running for my kit.

Ivan grins. "Sounds like dessert."

Anacine stacks our dishes in rapid order. "Just turn off the stupid coils and let's get inside."

Siff says, [Ivan, get one for dissection. I'm setting my blaster to taser.]

I agree with the call. A bloody battlefield is no victory. I set my blaster to stun as the iguanas hit us fast, tearing across the platform on all fours. I wait for the lead iguana and fire. The blaster hook vibrates inside its skin with an electric discharge strong enough to stun the creature's nervous system. When it doesn't stop I turn up the voltage. The iguana's head spins around like a propeller on a snake-like neck. Like carved gems, sparkling purple eyes move from the glowing coil to my blaster. It staggers off to the edge to crouch and watch.

Crystal and Siff set voltages high enough to leave iguanas twitching on the ground. Ivan fires one bullet and then switches to taser. Li'l Mike tackles a smaller iguana, riding it like a horse. Iguanas make no sound besides the clicking of talon fingers and toes on the platform. Junior Rangers shout initially, but as the one-sided battle continues we switch to heavy breathing and grunting.

Iguanas keep coming, twelve, fourteen, sixteen. We're going to use up taser barbs until Anacine turns off the heat lamps. As downed iguanas regain motor control they glare at us and jump over the side, sailing down to branches below. Not one of them checks on the dead iguana. Two of our heating lamps are lost in the raid. We gather by the Dragonfly to look over the body. The scaly quadruped has a hole drilled through the head between two giant purple eyeballs at the top. Ivan says, "Nice shot, if I do say so myself."

Anacine says, "Help me get it inside for the dissection."

"With such clean shot, Terra should see." Ivan pauses and then looks around. "My boots! They took my boots! I should have shot them all!"

Crystal says, "Quiet, I hear something."

We follow her across the platform, probing forest shadows with flashlights. Crystal stops at the edge near one of the huge columnar trees. With a metal finger she motions us around the trunk. From inside a hole, a baby iguana stares out at us, cradling one of Ivan's boots to its chest like a teddy bear. Crystal lifts it out by the webbing at its armpits. She holds it up to Ivan. "Here you go, killer. Are you going to step on it?"

Episode 5 – The Fall

Colonists are hit daily by floods as they labor to clear swampland. The Homestead's controlled burn left debris, and dams that fill and collapse unpredictably. Colonists try explosives to clear out mud and logs, but it churns the chum without much effect. The area is a mess.

Rangers and colony leaders fly out to visit our terrace farm. With added loads of soil, half the area is filled to a depth of five centimeters, and the platform shows no strain under the weight. We'll see if it holds when the dirt saturates with water under the next rain.

Ivan, Siff, Li'l Mike, and I have gone out several times to locate platforms, finding one about every fifteen square kilometers. On our island that would mean thirteen thousand platforms, and these are just platforms near the top. Below the canopy there could be many times that number of older platforms.

We don't know how or why they were built but we suspect that iguanas are the builders. They watch us constantly, stealing anything not nailed down. This has come to be known as the "iguana problem". We would hate to just wipe them out. We could almost certainly do it, but the best walking leaves no tracks.

Our colonists see themselves as good galactic citizens, not space invaders. Junior Rangers are expected to solve this problem, as if we haven't done our part already. We could build cages around the platforms but this would be difficult and costly. Iguanas move as easily in three dimensions as we do in two. For now we rig motion alarms in layers around the farm. Whenever they get too close we chase iguanas away with electric shocks.

When a signal is received, Siff, Crystal, Li'l Mike, and I move out. We have a system of swinging vines for Siff and I. Crystal uses her own cable and pulley arms. Li'l Mike scrambles along the trunks as easily as a spider. Ivan accuses us of playing cops and robbers instead of working the problem. I must admit the chases are exciting.

I think the iguanas provoke us for sport. As we chase them through the maze of trunks, iguanas flank us in three-dimensions. Where would iguanas learn classic military maneuvers? Maybe iguana tribes war with each other.

On the morning of day fifteen we wake in our own beds in the Dragonfly. After a shower I dress and join the others for breakfast on the platform. Colonists work the plot, tending crops from Earth. The skies above our green bowl are clear and bright, the morning air cool. Ivan warms his hands around a coffee. "I notice you no longer sleep outside, Thuy."

"I can hear the alarm just as well inside."

"Response time is slower."

"Security is my problem."

Crystal says, "Ivan's mad because he never found his other boot."

"Because you haven't found out where iguanas live. Find their nest and you will find our stuff."

"Maybe we're living on their nest already."

Ivan tilts his head listening to the jawbone. "It's Terra! Iguanas are attacking at south platform!"

We drop our plates, and run for the Dragonfly. South platform is eight kilometers away, about ten minutes by air. Siff and I ride outside on the skids, blasters set for bullets. Crystal readies the crane as we skim centimeters over treetops. The canopy above the southern platform is sparse but we haven't cut it away for easy access.

I code, [Siff, Li'l Mike, and I can ride the hook together. We'll need the firepower.]

Ivan says, [Forget it. I'm taking in Dragonfly.]

[The branches aren't cleared! You'll kill us all!]

[Then better jump off now. I'm going in.]

Siff codes, [Ivan, we'll get her.]

[She's in net! They're pulling her over side!]

Crystal codes, [If they get her into the trees we'll never catch up.]

[Thuy, get inside. Rig for crash landing!]

Ivan's face is grim as we dive towards a wall of green. "Switching to glide! Dropping rotor!"

The Dragonfly's wings pop to the sides, but we're going too slow for them to do much good. Rotor blades flip off, spinning away like Popsicle sticks as we rip through a tangle of leaves. The crash takes only seconds, branches grabbing the fuselage and turning us upside down. We drop nose-down, slamming into a heavy trunk.

The harness leaves bruises across my chest. The buckle is jammed so I pull Hackman from my boot sheath. As I cut through the straps, Junior Rangers groan around me. Li'l Mike crawls from body to body checking pulses. After the belt falls loose, I climb to the doorway. Fortunately the hatch isn't bent in the frame. [Everyone okay? I'm going out.]

Crystal codes, [Go.]

The other Junior Rangers are still dazed, but my first priority is Terra. Rangers stick together. I slide the door and stagger across a trunk towards the platform. Terra is bundled inside a net with one hand poking out. She holds desperately to a thin branch while iguanas push and pull at the netted ball.

When the stick finally snaps, the net slides over the edge. Terra screams as she falls. With blaster set to bullets I run to the edge of the platform. Terra dangles on a vine rope held by the iguanas. They're going to lower her down.

If I shoot the iguanas, she'll drop. If I don't shoot, they'll spirit her away through the mid-level maze. We'll never catch up. I learned that much from our chases. Crystal's voice appears in my head, [Ivan's unconscious. Siff and Anacine are okay. I'm coming out. What's your situation?]

[I can't shoot the iguanas or they'll drop Terra.]

[How far?]

I run a flashlight over a haystack of trunks sinking down forever. Terra would be a bloody meatball before she stuck on anything. [We have to let them have her. Where's Li'l Mike?]

The iguanas have stopped lowering. The light! When I swing the beam, purple crystalline eyes follow hypnotically on the end of smooth, light bulb shaped heads. From inside the net, Terra groans, "Give them your flashlight."

I set it on a trunk and back away. Now if only they don't drop the net. One of the iguanas with a broken tusk creeps forward. Talons bite nervously into the trunk. Others watch the proceedings. When their partner is within grabbing distance they tie off the rope. [It's a trade! They're giving us Terra for the flashlight! Smart!]

[I should think I'm worth a light pole at least.]

Eyes fastened on me the whole time, Half-tusk picks up the flashlight. As it looks into the beam, light reflects off the lenses of purple dodecahedra. The shapes must help iguanas see in the near-black of the forest. The iguana touches the glass cover and jumps, triggering jumps in human and iguanas alike.

Half-tusk turns its head to the others. With a whispered sound they jump off branches into the dark, using webbing at their sides to sail away. Iguanas stick to bark and jump again, escaping with my flashlight into the depths below.

Siff reaches the edge of the platform with a cable. [That is the weirdest thing I've ever seen.]

Terra wriggles in the net. "How's Ivan?"

[Broken nose, unconscious, but he has a strong pulse. If he didn't crash the Dragonfly you would be long gone. How are you doing?]

"Broken arm I think."

[Are you well enough to be pulled up?]

"Pull away. My arm's puffed and full of adrenaline. The real pain comes later when it softens."

As we reel the net, I say, "Have you seen Li'l Mike?"

"Here I am."

The mech crawls up the side of the trunk. It must have been directly under me for some time hanging upside down. "What were you doing there?"

"I thought I could reach the net."

"You couldn't hold it if you did."

"I wasn't planning to hold it. I was going to stick with Terra, in case you dropped it, or they took her away." Li'l Mike smiles reasonably. I think there's more he isn't saying.

An hour later we sit on South platform with the broken Dragonfly. Ivan holds his head, moaning, "She's gone! She'll never fly again."

Crystal says, "The machine shop can do amazing work."

Ivan yawns. "Wake me when she's ready."

He lays on the platform with the iguana net as a pillow. Anacine shakes his arm. "Ivan, don't go to sleep. You may have a concussion."

Ivan touches his nose. "Ouch! Is Gravitol, I think, shutting me down..."

As Ivan's eyes close, I say, "What set the iguanas off anyway?"

Terra cradles a cast on her wrist. "They were watching from the forest but they stayed away all night."

"What are you doing here?"

"Trying to measure the water cycle. Rain runs from the canopy to the swamp and out to sea. We want to figure out how it flows through the mid-level so we can intercept it for our farms."

"Down the hollow trunks?"

"So we think. I was pouring water marked with a radioactive tracer into that hollow trunk by the edge. I was going to rope down with a Geiger counter and find out where it went but the iguanas came after me with a net. I think I'll save that experiment for later."

Crystal taps Terra's cast with a metal finger. "The mission is over for you, mon."

"I may not be able to climb trees but I can still think. Junior Rangers can be my arms."

Ivan snorts in his sleep, wakes briefly, and drifts off again. As Terra looks on tenderly I just figured out my revenge for Ivan's needling.

We spend the afternoon on South platform gathering what we can from the wreckage of the Dragonfly. With cables and blocks we get her tipped and leveled on the platform. If we can't use the Dragonfly anymore, at least colonists will have a secure outpost. Ivan wants to clear branches overhead so we can lift her out with the Black Widow, but Lieutenant Nofree wants to look it over first.

After hours of hot work under the musty air of the canopy, Junior Rangers take a nap inside the Dragonfly. I close my eyes with the rest but lay still, heart hammering in my chest. In my career I've calmly faced alien teeth of every conceivable shape. That's nothing compared to the social embarrassment of getting caught playing a practical joke.

When every muscle in the cabin is still, I use my long practice at stealth, crawling to Terra's side with a red, felt-tipped pen. Holding my breath, I draw on her cast a large heart and the words inside, "Ivan loves Terra."

As I crawl back to my bunk, the blue of Anacine's open eyes sparkle. She winks once and closes them again. I ease myself into my bunk and close my eyes as well. In the short history of the colony project I wonder if one Junior Ranger has ever killed another? Out in the deadly environments we explore who would ever know? I fall asleep, waking later to Terra's squeals, "Ivan! I love you too!"

I lay still, watching through squinted eyes as Ivan wakes in a daze to Terra's smothering kisses. "Wha... What's going on?"

Terra holds her cast out proudly for all to see. "Isn't he the most romantic man you've ever seen!"

Crystal snickers, "Ivan? Romantic?"

Ivan sits up holding head and nose. He turns beet red as we wait for a statement. Ivan shrugs and mutters, "Is nothing." As Terra hugs him tight, Ivan looks over her shoulder measuring each of us, wheels turning behind cold black eyes.

Lieutenant Nofree isn't happy having to pick us up with the Black Widow. Saving Terra is doing our duty. Breaking the Dragonfly is unforgivable. If both Dragonfly and Black Widow are disabled, Rangers won't be going home. If one is put out of action the other has to cut back on risky missions. That means almost everything.

While the Black Widow hovers, Lieutenant Nofree yells at us. Bravo Top rides a cable to inspect the Dragonfly. When the big Link fires the engines to check for cracks the platform doesn't even budge. It's like cement. Tank says, "Where are the propellers?"

Ivan points over the side. "I had to drop them or Dragonfly would have been knocked off course."

"Crystal, go down and see if they're in one piece."

"Sir."

"Ivan, what's wrong with the engines?"

"Jet intake blades were trashed by branches. Do you think she can be fixed?"

"We'll try. Off the record, Rangers appreciate what you did."

Ivan nods. Would he have done the same for a Ranger he wasn't dating? Lieutenant Nofree gets in a few more threats while the Dragonfly is readied for lifting. As the Widow flies away with the Dragonfly dangling underneath, Ivan puts a protective arm around Terra's shoulders.

While the Dragonfly is back at the Homestead for repairs, Terra and the Junior Rangers are assigned to start a second farm on South platform. After tangling with iguana nets we don't like sleeping outdoors. We have our kits, light poles, alarms, and loads of mud dumped into the middle of the planking. Even if Ivan laughs at me, I wear body armor again. I'm not the one with a broken nose.

The first farm is growing well with soil suspended above the pool in troughs, but colonists would like to build their own platforms wherever they want. They think it's too dangerous spreading out in clans over a hundred square kilometers. They'd like to turn branches into roads and walkways through the trees. As part of the Junior Ranger's assignment, we're to figure out how iguanas melt those living branches together, if indeed they are the builders.

Ivan has the bright idea of setting out light poles as bait and following them back to the iguana's lair. Maybe we'll find some kind of wood morphing device in their garage. We attach transmitters to the poles, and while waiting for an attack, we go about transforming the terrace into a farm.

Before dinner we wash mud from our hands with a hose attached to a hanging water tank. Crystal sits on the ground with a rag and one leg in her lap. "I shouldn't have gone with steel, mon. I sink right through the mud to my rusting ankles. In the next shipment I'll send for my skeletor frame and flat, rubber feet. If the Dragonfly were here..."

Ivan says, "Don't blame me for inconvenience. Dragonfly is being repaired and Rangers owe us debt."

Siff says, [Lieutenant Nofree thinks we could have saved Terra from the hook.]

"There was no time!"

[*We* know that. The other Rangers think you were just showing off for your girlfriend.]

"Rangers can kiss my foot. Hey, look at that!"

An iguana stands on hind feet, holding light poles in either claw. It swivels a snake-thin head from one pole to the other as if deciding which to take. Siff says, [Thuy, the motion alarm.]

I put on pogs to read data in the air. "Nothing. It must have been here before I turned on the sensors."

[That was an hour ago.]

Crystal quietly slips on her leg. "It's taking its sweet time, mon. Are the poles transmitting?"

I switch displays to pole data. "Loud and clear. We just have to follow them home."

Siff says, [I'll get it started.] He shouts, "Hey you! Thtop!"

The iguana drops one of the poles, tucks the other into the webbing under its arm, and scrambles on three limbs over the edge. The motion sensor in my head finally starts to beep. The perimeter has been breached. Why didn't it go off before? I grab Li'l Mike's hand and take off. "Come on, Rangers! Triangulate!"

We leap long distances in the low gravity of Klondike-2, but the iguana outpaces us. It travels horizontally in the shadowed light of canopy and then starts down. Siff yells, "There, by that column."

"I see it. Are there two of them now?"

Siff looks with his fake eye. [I don't think so. How's the signal?]

"It's getting lost bouncing around the trunks. Tie a rope. We have to go down fast." I pat the mech on the back. "Go! Follow the signal!"

Li'l Mike starts down like a squirrel circling the trunk. Siff gets a rope from his kit, and we rappel down through the dark mid-level. After several minutes we can no longer see it, but the pole transmitter shows the iguana still moving down.

As I run across a horizontal trunk my foot catches and I fall face first, nearly sliding over the side. Siff jogs behind to help me up. [Good thing you kept your armor.]

Heart pounding by the close call, I look back to see what tripped me. In a globe of light from our kits, lizard-birds are trapped in nets in surrounding branches. Some still flap weakly. [A pantry. We must be getting close.]

I cut sticky webbing off my boot. "As long as we don't become part of the pantry. Uh-oh, signal's gone."

[The others are behind me. Should we wait?]

"Li'l Mike's going to get lost. Let's keep at it. You go down at a sixty-degree angle, I'll go down at thirty. The iguana should be somewhere in that envelope." I talk in my throat, [Keep in contact with the jawbone radio.]

[Loud and clear], Siff codes. He gives a thumbs-up and jogs along the branch.

I tie a rope from my kit and drop. How am I ever going to maintain a sixty-degree descent? Minutes later Siff codes, [Got a signal. Move further east.]

[Roger.] I drop to a flat branch and jog horizontally until the pole transmitter starts to beep. [Got it. We're closing in. Li'l Mike, are you here?]

No answer.

Siff says, [Sorry, lost it again. Thuy? It must be moving toward you.]

[We'll flush it into a dead end yet. Move down.]

[We're not trying to flush it. We're trying to find its nest.]

I wonder why there's only one. They usually travel in groups. Is this chase part of a counter-strategy? I tightrope along a thin branch, keeping one eye on pog data and one eye on jumping light and shadows from my blaster light. The pole transmitter beeps louder for proximity.

I set the blaster on taser, and in that brief moment, miss my footing. I collapse the other knee to lower my center of gravity. My foot swings down hard to bang the tree and pull me upright. It doesn't work; I lean over faster.

From above my head a net flies down hard as if thrown. I grasp tough fibers and jerk down to regain my balance but the net gives. Both net and I go over the side. I wrap my arm and leg through the netting in case it's tied somewhere further up.

Jolting to a stop, I nearly lose my blaster. I dangle on the net, too surprised to question its origin. I shine a flashlight below me a long way down, and above, a taut vine from net to branch. At the top of the branch iguanas look down with purple dodecahedra eyes flashing in the light. Maybe it *was* a trap. They could have flanked us and been moving down all around us to our sides.

[Siff, I'm in a net.]

[Animals!]

[No, they saved me, at least temporarily. I was falling and they threw a net.]

[Are you okay?]

[Hanging on by a thread. There's no way down and I got iguanas up top.]

[Don't let go. I'm on my way.]

Cradling the blaster in one arm I climb to the top of the net. I wrap my legs tight and sling the blaster to my back. There's no question of shooting them now. I loosen my knife in its ankle sheath. As I prepare to climb the rope hand over hand, another net is readied. They mean to catch me! [Siff, the natives may not be friendly.]

[What's going on, old buddy?]

[A second net. You may have to look for me in the pantry. I'll fire a few rounds to scare them off.]

I set the blaster to bullets, shooting at a trunk above the iguana's heads. I can't hit them through their perch but they might be stung with flying chips. The iguanas are unimpressed. The net is thrown, nearly knocking my blaster away. It glances off my shoulder and is reeled up again.

We can't go on this way. Iguanas seem to value light so I spray a nearby branch with flaming jellied gasoline. The iguanas screech with excitement. [Siff, any closer?]

[About two hundred meters. Hang on.]

[Look for the campfire and bring marshmallows.]

The blaster doesn't stop the iguanas. It may even increase their determination to catch me. As other nets are readied, Li'l Mike creeps down the trunk above the iguana's heads. [Li'l Mike, tie off the rope!]

The mech makes eye contact but says nothing. [Li'l Mike! Can you hear?]

He looks over his shoulder at Siff's approaching light. Li'l Mike's radio may be out. "Mike, stall them just a few more seconds."

The mech stares at me as one of the nets flies down hitting my blaster. I'll have to stall them myself. I sweep a wave of flame just touching the outer edge of the other net. The material flares and crackles catching fire. Add iguana nets to the resources colonists can use for fuel.

The iguana screams and lets the net loose. It flutters down to me like a flaming butterfly wrapping around my vine. Oops. I whip out my knife to fling the burning net away. The vine holding me chars, crackles, and snaps. Elevator going down, glad I wore armor. [Siff, I'm falling. Look for me in the swamp.]

I can't sub vocalize as my head is knocked from branch to branch. Flailing arms and legs, I lose my blaster and kit. They fall faster than me through the sieve of branches. Instincts war within me. Pull limbs tight so they stop slamming branches versus extending limbs to catch the branches and slow my fall.

Siff yells, [Thuy, I see the flames. Hang on, I'm coming. What's your situation? I see iguanas. There's our light pole. Do you think they led us into a trap? Thuy, what's your situation?]

[Down!] I croak.

The mech is not troubled by orders to kill one of the Junior Rangers. Survival often entails killing, and Li'l Mike is a survival machine. The problem is murdering without bringing suspicion on himself. Doc Blaitel was very specific about that.

As the mission proceeds, Li'l Mike looks for opportunities to be alone with one or another of the Junior Rangers. A slip here or shove there and it would all be over. The planet itself provides deadly challenges without the mech's intervention. That would be best. So far, Junior Rangers have escaped fatalities.

Li'l Mike is to replace one of the Junior Rangers. Part of his assignment is to decide which should die in order to build the strongest team. It's a complex problem. Junior Rangers each have strengths and weaknesses. The mech gives rankings based on strength, intelligence, speed, skills, and personality. The rankings don't put one clearly on the bottom. After two weeks, and with time running out, Li'l Mike decides that any one of them will do.

When Ivan crashes the Dragonfly into South platform, Junior Rangers are knocked out and hanging from their belts. As he climbs around the hold checking for pulses the mech thinks his job might be done. They are all alive but the jerk of a belt across one of their necks could finish the job. Unfortunately, Thuy is conscious and Thuy knows that the others are alive as well. A broken neck at this point would be suspicious. Li'l Mike decides to wait for a better chance.

Whenever they enter the forest, Li'l Mike commits maximum processing power to audio/visual sensors. Junior Rangers are often forced to split up. In his pocket Li'l Mike carries part of a tusk he broke off one of the lizard creatures. If he finds himself alone with a Ranger, one hard jab with the tooth would split a carotid wide open. The Ranger would be dead before they could take a breath to yell. Li'l Mike's story of an iguana attack would be believed.

When Ivan comes up with the plan to track stolen light poles through the forest, Li'l Mike makes sure that he's always ready to go. Junior Rangers will be alone and stretched out over hundreds of meters.

It doesn't take long for the plan to commence. Li'l Mike sticks with Thuy and Siff as they race ahead of the others on the track of an iguana. Although he's told to track the thief, Li'l Mike paces Thuy to the sides looking for a chance to pounce. The humans are pitifully slow, stringing ropes and picking their way carefully across horizontal runs.

At any time the iguana could sail away without effort, bouncing from branch to branch with the stolen light. When it does not, Li'l Mike realizes that the humans are being led away purposefully. This is confirmed when the mech catches glimpses of iguanas pacing them to the sides.

If iguanas were to actually kill one of the Junior Rangers, it would completely remove suspicion from Li'l Mike. After the deed is done, the mech will hurl his unneeded broken tooth down through the maze. Only one of the Junior Rangers is to die. Li'l Mike might even have to save others after the first one is killed.

It doesn't take long before Thuy hangs from a net. Li'l Mike creeps down over the iguana's heads wondering why they don't finish the job. If the iguanas won't kill him, Li'l Mike could knock them aside. A fall would kill Thuy as surely as talons and teeth.

While the mech considers, bullets chew up branches around him. Li'l Mike jumps behind the tree, planning ways to accelerate the process. Siff is getting closer. Incapable of remorse, Li'l Mike ignores the Ranger's pleas through his jawbone radio.

The mech looks into Thuy's eyes, and prepares to leap onto an iguana's back and cut the rope. Thuy sprays a fountain of fire. The net chars and down Thuy goes. The broken tooth is sent tumbling after. Li'l Mike prepares to save Siff but iguanas jump off into the forest like a gang of flying squirrels.

Episode 6 – Half-Tusk

I don't know how far I fell. I have trouble even remembering my name. It's pitch black, cold. Silence greets my jawbone radio. Stretched between moist branches of wood my body is puffed and sore. Probably broke every vein within a centimeter of the surface. The kit and blaster are gone. My little watch light shows only a meter into the darkness, a dripping swampy location. I don't think I'm down as far as bedrock. Artificial molecules spill into my bloodstream bringing relief. At least I have the leech.

[Siff?] I code. No answer.

The watch stack that has greater range. I hit the transmitter. "Siff?"

"Thank goodneth! We got a fix on you, old buddy. We were afraid your watch got ripped off."

"Nope, I rode it all the way down. How soon can you get me?"

"Crythtal ith coming with pulleyth and rope. Three hourth?"

"Three hours! It took me only ten minutes."

"Ouch, a ten minute beating. Hang in there. You got your kit?"

"I threw it away. I didn't think I'd need it."

"Okay, don't get thor."

"Sorry, I think I used up all my Gravitol supply."

"About that, Thuy. I know it mutht hurt but the leth Gravitol the better. After Ivan broke hith nowth the Gravitol kicked in and he couldn't thtay awake."

"I do feel sleepy." I unbuckle the strap, holding the stack's microphone to my mouth. "I took off the leech but chemicals are already in my blood. Hurry."

"We're coming, Thuy. Hang on for a few hourth."

"Right. Thuy, out."

A few hours seems optimistic. When we roped down the other day it took four. It takes time to secure the pulleys. Still, things could be worse. When I take off my skids to see how much worse, I'm surprised to find my knife in its sheath.

I flung the burning net away with the blade just before I fell. Somehow I got the knife back into its sheath as the first blows rained down. A miracle? Or was it training guiding my actions unconsciously, like an honest man that doesn't have to consider every word he speaks.

Discarded body armor forms a line along the branch: helmet, gloves, forearm, bicep, shoulder, chest, and back plates. The top half of my torso is one big bruise. I know the lower half is worse. Hoping the feeling will return, I've been ignoring the fact that I can't move my left leg.

I take off boots, ankle knife, right calf, right femur cladding... I can stall no longer. The left tibia is broken. At least no bone pokes out from the skin. If I hadn't been wearing skids I wouldn't have enough bone fragments to pin together.

A broken leg would keep me in the Dragonfly the remaining two weeks on Klondike-2: hot showers, soft bed, and no farmer's calluses on my poor bruised hands. I smile and try to stay awake. The pain isn't too bad if I don't move.

Neurotransmitters soak into my tissues like plum sauce. After those break down I'll be in agony. It's so dark my brain thinks it's nighttime. Gravitol is pulling me down. When the branch shakes, my eyes fly open. I reach for my watch, patting along the moist wood. "Li'l Mike?" I whisper hopefully.

In the cast of my watch light, giant purple eyes stare back. Nose slits open to smell with a soft whuffing sound. This one must be from a different tribe than the net throwers up top. Could they climb down this fast? I let the light blink off when the iguana reaches towards my watch.

The branch shakes again with another iguana. Terror rises in my throat. The scaly reptilian creatures hiss to each other. I click the light on to find one examining the chest plate. "Go away!" I scream.

The iguana looks at me with disdain, reaching again for my watch. I turn it off. Adrenaline that floods my body is scooped up by Gravitol. I must sleep. Ivan was right, Gravitol is too dangerous for a Delta Ranger. I can't move, can't fight. The iguanas have control but I can save my watch at least. I thread the strap through the buckle... so sleepy...

I wake shivering in pitch-blackness. It's silent except for the sounds of dripping water. I don't care what Siff says, I need more Gravitol to soothe screaming nerve endings. But didn't I already put on the leech? I feel my naked wrist in panic. Did I buckle it in time? Iguana fingers that can tie knots could certainly undo a buckle.

I feel along the branch. My skids, boots, and knife are gone as well. I have nothing... No, not nothing, I have a broken leg and indescribable pain. Where are the Junior Rangers? It feels like I've been asleep for hours.

[Hello?] At least iguanas can't steal the transmitter out of my jaw.

Junior Rangers should be here, following the watch. I hope those iguanas live nearby. When the Rangers find my watch they should be within range of the jawbone radio.

I lay back to assess the situation. Can I move? My leg is only cracked in one place. A splint will keep it from flopping. My kit! It fell on a similar trajectory, namely down. It could be within a dozen meters if the iguanas didn't find it. Or the strap could have hung up on one of a million sticks in the kilometer high forest over my head. Same with the blaster. I'd settle for either right now. How can I search without light?

Straddling a branch, broken leg hanging down in searing pain I scoot forward. The air is freezing cold but surprisingly the branch gives off warmth. I assumed that only the top layer of trees was really alive, building on the husks of dead ancestors. Trees in the canopy must feed solar energy to their parents while trees in the swamp feed water and minerals to their offspring.

The branch ends at a trunk so massive it seems to stretch like a wall to either side. I tap with my good leg feeling for the next branch down. The kit better be below me. If it's any higher it might as well be in Kathmandu.

I move down a staircase of branches. In the middle of blackness, points of light sparkle like stars in the distance. There are bioluminescent lizards in the swamp. I curse myself for not reading the reports. Are the lizards poisonous? Edible? Baby alligators?

If I could grab a few of those lizards, I wouldn't have to sweep fingers through every moldering pile of leaves searching for the kit. A handful of glowing lizards might attract predators, but anything down here already has excellent night vision. Any kind of light would give me a greater advantage.

While figuring out how to catch and hold the lizards, I reach bedrock. I've been in the swamp the whole time. Freezing water pools above the rock, trickling away through massive clumps of roots. Are there swamp fish I could eat? Too soon to think about that. The Junior Rangers will be here soon. I might need water though.

I sit in the pool letting icy water numb my legs as good as any Gravitol. I lay back to wash away blood, sweat, and grit from my jumpsuit. It feels like a wintry tomb. I could close my eyes, fall asleep, and never be seen again. I'd be just another human swallowed by the hostile universe, the last of the original Junior Rangers.

Would the others remember my face the way I remember all those Junior Rangers that passed before me? The Rangers would cluck their tongues and say that my luck finally ran out. No, I think bitterly. If I go, I won't go quietly.

In the water are broken branches too long to negotiate the tangle of roots to float away. I select two about the length of my lower leg. I find flexible roots that would make good ties, but I can't rip them from the root ball. I chop with jagged sticks for a while and then feel along the bottom. Where taproots of massive trees plunge through bedrock are smaller chips that I can work loose.

Sawing with a sharp rock wedge I cut roots to get a reasonable splint assembled around my leg. Feeling more like a Delta Ranger I feel through the water for my kit or blaster. If I get some light I'll expand the search outward in a spiral. There's no question of going higher. With a broken leg and the pounding I took on the way down I don't have the strength to step or pull.

My ancestors used to keep giant crickets. Not insects, but pets that would crawl around the house, returning at night to their bamboo cages. I chop out more of the roots to weave a cage about the size of a beach ball. Now for the hard part, catching my bioluminescent pets. I don't see any around.

I should keep moving but my body is sore and getting sorer by the minute. I struggle to climb tangled roots above the freezing pool and fold wet sticks into a nest. Inside my aching head I code, [Siff? Anybody?]

I lay my broken leg as flat as possible to relieve the pressure and close my eyes. When a swish-swish moves through the water, I code cautiously, [Siff? Is that you?]

I reach silently for my knife before remembering it's gone, along with watch and body armor. I lean over my platform of sticks to stare down at the water. In pitch blackness, phantom squiggles of purple and yellow flash in my eyes. A faint white line is located by sound as much as the trace of photons leaking off the creature's back.

Three meters long, the line slides smoothly through the water as the creature continues its daily hunt for prey. It has to be an alligator like those that attacked us on the river. This one is bigger, hopefully too big to climb to my platform. It's a foolish wish; I must prepare to climb or fight.

I try to remember if the other alligators had noses. Can the beast smell me? Does it hunt by sound or sight? There's no mud around so I don't think I'm in its nest. Maybe it will just move on. I tense my broken leg to see if it's in any shape for climbing. The pain that answers back is so intense I nearly cry out. No climbing.

If the alligator locates me I'll have to fight. Visualizing the creatures from the river I fit myself onto its back, arms wrapped around the neck out of reach of the teeth. My one good leg will have to do, hooked under the beast's rear leg. My broken leg will flop like a stick dragging on a string behind a car. No help for it. If I pass out from the pain, I'm done for anyway.

I have the fist-sized jagged rock in my pocket. I doubt I could saw through skin on the beast's thick neck, but the alligator might get so annoyed by the attempt that it moves on. Perhaps sensing something, the creature pauses beneath my platform.

Running my finger along the jagged rock edge I think about flinging it away for the hunter to chase. I dismiss the idea, sensing the splash would arouse something deep in the beast's reptilian brain. It's both experience and intuition that marks me as a survivor of countless worlds.

And just as quickly as it appeared the creature swims on. I wonder what in my presence caused it to pause? Body heat? In the dark I can't be sure. I wait, angry and tense for another half hour before falling into a troubled sleep, the finish of a full day alone on Klondike-2.

Why do we never appreciate good health until it's gone? Why don't I wake up in my cot every morning, breathe deeply, and rejoice to be alive? Why do I condemn the hurts and never praise good health? I assume that my smooth functioning body is the normal state of things. It's not. We are vast networks of biochemical systems, and the breakdown of any one of these is enough to throw the body into a downward spiral of disease.

If I get out of this alive I won't moan so much over a paper cut. Getting out alive may be a problem. Junior Rangers should have found me long ago. Something is seriously wrong. A massive iguana attack?

The more I think about it the more I think iguanas led us away on purpose. We know almost nothing about their level of intelligence except that they can tie knots and build toys. Could they pick us off one by one?

I have no watch alarm to wake me, and don't know how long I slept. The Junior Rangers could have come and gone. I think I would have heard their voices inside my head. I'm extremely sore but restless, unaccountably cheered by a number of soft glowing lines nearby. Without my splashing around, bioluminescent lizards have returned.

I tighten the splint and climb down to the rock to drink and retrieve my cage. Stepping quietly through the water I sneak up on the first lizard. My hand shoots out to grab it around the soft middle. Slightly disappointed that it doesn't put up a fight, I drop it in the basket and weave the hatch closed to see if it's tight.

When the lizard doesn't thrash around testing the seams I have to shake the cage to see if it falls out. I adjust a few links and then like an apple picker, grab more of the creatures to feed the basket. With glowing lizards I can see into the swamp around me, not far but I'll have some warning if something tries to sneak up.

Holding the basket in one hand I hop around columns of roots searching for my kit or blaster among drifts of leaves, piles of mud and rock, and into deeper pools of water. I follow a growing spiral, alert for the smells of an alligator nest. My broken leg is often in freezing water and too numb to feel. I fear the pain will return if I have to climb out of the water.

I don't find my things, but among thousands of sticks I find two decent crutches with flat ends for my armpits. After an hour's limping search I enter a clearing. It's hard to believe there's a forest stretching a kilometer overhead. A dam on the low water side of the clearing holds a pool about a meter deep.

At the very limit of the caged lizard light I can make out a flat wood ceiling that has the melted look of a platform. There's no way I could climb on top, but sinking down from the platform are mysterious waves of heat.

I decide to make this base camp without knowing exactly where I am. It's not too far from where I dropped, and it's been at least half a day since I lost contact. I can no longer assume the Junior Rangers will come to my rescue. If I'm to live I'll have to stay warm. The air beneath the wooden roof is not as cold as elsewhere in the swamp. There are loose sticks I can stack in a pile to make a bed. There are bioluminescent fish to eat if I have to stay more than a few days.

I hang the lizard cage from a branch. As I pile sticks to get above freezing water I feel a presence. It's not the primal terror of teeth and blood, but a benign intelligence, watchful, curious. [Li'l Mike?] I code.

I continue working, sneaking peeks out of the corners of my eyes. Finally I spot an iguana looking down from the far edge of the ceiling. I give up the act and look directly. The iguana with half a tusk stares at me like it owns the place. "Well, thief? Where's my light pole?"

Actually, I'm hugely relieved. If the pole and transmitter are nearby the Rangers won't be far behind. "Your ancestors built this platform, didn't they?" It could be tens or hundreds of thousands of years old. With a sense of awe I walk the edges looking for a way up. Half-tusk watches but doesn't move until I get a few meters away. I think it's impressed by my hanging lizard lantern.

Unfortunately, I can find no way to reach the ceiling overhead and can't guess what produces those falls of heat. I'm tired and my pallet of sticks is ready. I'll sleep awhile. If the Rangers don't get here soon I'll try to climb a tree and rope down to the platform.

When I wake my lizard cage is gone. No, the lizards sleep too. When I shake the cage the light comes on. If I'm still here tomorrow I'll let these go and collect fresh bulbs. Half-tusk is back, watching from the shadows. Holding something in its claws it stares at me as if trying to make up its mind. "Food?" I say hopefully.

Half-tusk creeps closer, wading through the pool beneath the platform. It touches my lizard cage and then holds out a stick, my knife! I move slowly so as not to frighten it. The sheath is gone but it's Hackman all right, handle cracked from the fall. As I take the knife, I say, "Not to be ungrateful or anything, but have you found my kit or blaster?"

The iguana stares out of two gemstone eyes from the top of its small, egg-shaped head. When it turns to leave, I say, "Wait."

Half-tusk turns back while I fumble for the jagged rock in my pocket. From the way it shattered in razor-sharp planes, I guess that the rock is like flint from Earth. Made of sand, compressed and reheated in magma, flint is especially hard, hard enough to knock iron atoms out of steel. I hold the rock in one hand and whack it with the butt of the knife. It sends out a shower of sparks, iron atoms combusting with oxygen in the air.

Like an appreciative child at a puppet show, Half-tusk jumps up and down. I knock it a couple more times brightening the clearing with flashes. When Half-tusk reaches for the knife, I say, "Wait, watch this."

I can't set dense Klondike-2 wood on fire but I can get some dead leaves to smoke. I hold the knife at an angle to a leafy stick on the edge of my platform. After sharp strikes, the leaves smoke and then burst into flame. The fire spreads to the wood, and the corner of my pallet's on fire! "Look at that!" I cry, holding up a fiery stick. "We got fuel for the colonists!"

I expect some response, but Half-tusk is gone. My raving scared it off. I dismiss the iguana, we have fuel for the colonists! But what makes this wood different from wood up top that we can't burn? It's been soaking in swamp water under the pallet, maybe for thousands of years. Is that the difference? I know the answer is here somewhere.

Klondike-2 wood can be made to burn. Like a thief exploring a castle dungeon I hold the proof blazing in my hand. Even if colonists have to gather sticks from the swamps there's enough to last centuries. Now if I can only get back to tell them.

My own life has taken on new importance. I can save the colony. Before I attempt the long climb back, I must see what's on top of the platform. I take my crutches and circle the area, finding a trunk with low branches. I cut a root with my knife, and loop it around my head and shoulders like a garden hose. I tie the lantern to hang behind my head leaving both hands free to climb.

Dragging a splinted leg, I hoist myself up ten meters. It's higher than I intended to climb but it looks like branches have been purposely cleared around the platform. As well as a floor there are walls and a ceiling to this platform. It's a little hut, and a tantalizing red glow flickers through cracks in the wood.

I have to work halfway around the structure to find an overhanging branch. I tie off the root and lower myself to a narrow ledge. As I sidestep along the wall, streams of heated air flow through cracks. It's like a smokehouse, perhaps treating wood so it will burn.

Reaching a small opening in the structure, my theory changes. In the center of the room is a pile of flat rocks built into an oven. Stacks of firewood line the walls and scattered around the floor are spherical white eggs the size of softballs.

"It's a bakery," I say, licking my lips. It's been a long time since I've eaten. I lift one of the leather shells, shaking it like a birthday present. A thumping sound indicates a form inside too advanced for comfortable eating. I set it down and find one that's solid, yolk not yet consumed by a growing creature.

These must be alligator eggs, iguanas raid their nests. I sit on the floor with the egg in my lap. Heat from the fire drives away a swampy chill. After the meal I may try to get a quick nap in here. Iguanas have shown no hostility so far and would surely share their smokehouse.

I try to poke a hole with a stick. The shell is as tough as an old shoe. When I raise the stick to stab, iguanas scramble through the door. Hissing and baring fangs I can't doubt their deadly intent. I roll the egg away and raise my hands. I'm not that hungry anyway.

While the hostile creatures guard me, a small one puts the egg back into the pile. You would think they could spare one from the batch. Maybe their boss counts. I pick up my lantern and back away limping. With the heat of the room comes easier blood circulation and greater pain in my leg. I back to the doorway.

As I turn along the narrow ledge to reach my vine, I'm hit full-force by an iguana. I fall to the pool, gasping with shock in the icy water. Such is their anger I wouldn't be surprised to hear splashes of pursuit. Iguanas on the platform block the door, glaring down. I retrieve my crutches and cage. I wade beneath their platform and hop away through the swamp like a cast off hobo.

The jawbone radio cuts off. Li'l Mike assumes that Thuy's skull has been ground to mush as it bangs down through the endless maze of trees. Junior Rangers gather around the spot where he fell. Siff recounts what happened. The mech adds detail, purposefully edging his way into the circle. Through her tears, Anacine says, "I can't believe he's gone."

Li'l Mike says, "I tried to grab the rope."

Crystal pats the mech's back. "We know you did, mon. We know you did."

Ivan says, "We'll need to retrieve body. We'll take him back to moon."

Crystal tries the jawbone a few times and then switches to the watch radio. "No answer, but the watch survived. From the GPS signal it looks like he made it all the way to the swamp."

Siff nods with barely suppressed rage. [If Rangers won't put his name on the honor wall, I'll sneak in and carve it myself!]

Anacine says, "He was probably knocked out quickly. He didn't suffer."

"Siff?" the voice whispers from Siff's watch.

Siff checks the directory. "It'th Thuy! Hee'th alive!"

Crystal says, "Don't just stand there gaping, mon. Answer him."

Siff cries out in joy, "Thank goodneth! We got a fix on you, old buddy. We were afraid your watch got ripped off."

The mech doesn't get frustrated. There's no program for that. Li'l Mike takes inputs from sensors to build the most accurate model of the world that he can. Doc Blaitel directs what the world *should* look like. Interactive programs set goals to push the world from here to there. One of the Junior Rangers must die, Thuy is not dead. Therefore Li'l Mike must kill Thuy or one of the others.

Thuy must have been badly damaged in the fall and might die on his own. Li'l Mike decides to wait. Two dead Junior Rangers is not in the desired model.

Receiving data from Thuy's leech, Junior Rangers know how badly he's been hurt. The rescue attempt begins immediately. They have to climb back to the Dragonfly to grab all the rope and pulleys they can carry. Ivan locks the door. By the time they start down an hour later Siff's watch is on the move. Crystal checks data in her pogs. "The leech is off his wrist but the watch is heading east."

Siff says, [I wouldn't be surprised if he broke the buckle on the way down.]

Anacine thumbs the radio. "Thuy, do you read? Thuy?"

Ivan says, "Maybe he broke hearing as well. Do we follow watch?"

Crystal says, "That's a problem, mon. Do we assume a constant rate of travel east over the hours it's going to take to get down?"

Anacine says, "Where's he going anyway? You think the iguanas got him?"

Impatient to save his friend, Siff says, [Let's just climb. We'll change the angle as we go.]

Junior Rangers agree, returning to where Thuy fell. Li'l Mike paces them to the side using tree trunks to climb rather than cables or ropes. A hundred meters down they find Thuy's kit impaled on a branch. Siff shakes his head. [Thuy's going to have a cold night.]

Thuy's watch continues slowly moving east and then heads northeast. When they take a break two hours later, Ivan says, "We have to make decision. Thuy keeps moving, and we can't match angle. Do we move sideways now or keep dropping and try to walk through swamp?"

Crystal says, "Thuy is moving easily enough. I say we get down as fast as we can and try to pick up his trail."

"Fast as we can is still three of four hours."

Anacine says, "He's got to stop soon and sleep. Maybe he's moving to keep warm."

Siff says, [If the iguanas aren't forcing him to march. Let's drop faster.]

Ivan nods and they keep heading down. No one asks for Li'l Mike's opinion. If they had sent him on alone the mech would have already been there. Hoping that the injured Thuy would die without medical assistance, Li'l Mike doesn't volunteer. On the other hand, if the mech got there first he could finish Thuy off. As Junior Rangers string out along their cable system, Li'l Mike moves to the side, getting lost in the pitch black forest.

The Junior Rangers can't make contact long past the time when they should have been in range of the jawbone radio. Six hours after he fell, Thuy's watch stops moving. Crystal says, "He either dropped the watch or dropped in his tracks."

When they reach mountains of moldering vegetation, the signal from Thuy's watch is only a hundred meters away. As they wade through standing water and climb over piles of roots, Crystal points out talon marks along the trail. "Iguanas, but no boot prints."

From a pile of mushed fruit, Anacine pulls out a curved white plate. "One of Thuy's skids. There's blood along the edge."

Siff points out a light ahead. [There he is! There he is!]

Junior Rangers push through tangles of roots to see a figure standing on the ground next to a pile of skids. The mech turns, and holds up Thuy's watch. "The buckle's not broken."

Junior Rangers look for Thuy inside the freezing dark. Roots arch overhead like the ribs of a skeleton. Li'l Mike shakes his head. "No sign of a body."

As I limp towards my nest of sticks, I curse the Junior Rangers for abandoning me. I thought we were family. I wouldn't give up on them. Just like the colonists I'm starting over on a new world and need basic resources: food, energy, water, security, movement. I'm my own alphabet soup: alpha, bravo, charlie, delta, echo. I must find a way to climb a thousand meters with a broken leg. That, or plan for a short, nasty life far from sunlight in the swamp.

I open my lantern cage and throw out lizards that have been growing dim. They need to feed and recharge. I catch more by the time I reach my old nest. I sit in the dim light, shivering and growing angrier by the minute. I'm tempted to eat one of the lizards, a declaration of independence from my former team. Something terrible must have happened.

As I contemplate my friend's fate, I chop Hackman on a thick root: chunk, chunk, chunk. I vary the rhythm, tapping out a song I made up years ago,

> Hackman fever, nah, nah, nah-nah.
> Chopping like a cleaver, nah, nah, nah-nah.
> Stabbing like a wreaver, nah, nah, nah-nah.
> Hackman fever, nah, nah, nah-nah.
> Chewing like a beaver, nah, nah, nah-nah.
> Hackman fever, nah...

I'm startled when the root breaks through. What am I doing? Leading a parade? Every alligator within five hundred meters is probably headed this way. I need to be smart now. If this is to be my home I'll need a permanent fire. I have my knife. I can trap an alligator and skin it for blankets or a coat. I have fresh water and fish. When my leg heals I can climb high enough to find melons and squirrel meat.

What kind of life would this be, all alone in a pitch-black forest of ancient tree trunks? I could work my way to the coast or build my home on a platform. I could even take over the iguana egg house. They're fearsome enough with claws and fangs, but if I set traps and made it my focus, how long could they resist?

So I would be master of an egg house and no one to talk to. Once you're past the point of survival, what's left? Animals survive out of instinct. That's enough for them. Humans need goals bigger than themselves. Maybe I could befriend the iguanas. They're intelligent, Half-tusk seems nice. I don't anticipate evening meals around the dining table with stimulating conversation, but they might let me skulk around the outer edge of iguana society. I could play marbles with the kids like some half-wit uncle.

Yes, that's enough for now. As my stomach growls in the dark I think they may even let me have one of their baked alligator eggs. Before I can start winning them over, I have to find out what happened to the colony. What befell my friends that they couldn't rescue me? I have to climb out; I cut long roots.

Sticking close to the trunk I heave myself from one branch to the next. When I reach a gap I throw a knotted root to the next level. Sometimes it sticks and sometimes not. If it does I haul myself up hand over hand. If not I move sideways. Some of the gaps are too big to bridge.

After an hour's excruciating work I've climbed ten meters. It's hopeless, but at least I tried. I need to wait for my leg to heal. I scramble down and soak my leg in freezing water until it's numb again.

I climb onto my nest. With rock and knife I try to get a pile of sticks to light. I strike them over and over sending showers of sparks but none of them catch. Apparently, soaking the sticks in swamp water is not the answer. Why do those near the platform catch fire and not mine?

I should go back to the platform and steal some firewood. I have to if I don't want to freeze to death. When I cast my eyes in the direction of the platform, two eyes stare back. Half-tusk! Iguanas sent someone to guard against my return. It's not fair, I was only going to eat one.

When Half-tusk sees me looking, he... it... she moves closer. From the gentle way the creature moves, I decide it's female. Half-tusk chews through a root from the tree. I grip the broken handle on my knife, and scoot back in my nest.

She stops within scratching distance, perching on a branch. Half-tusk takes the stick I had been trying to light. With the torn end of the root she rubs the stick, mashing sap into the surface. She does the same with a curl of bark and throws the root away. Half-tusk looks at me with deep-purple eyes centered on the top of her head. I think she wants to make sure I'm watching as she sets the bark on the edge of my nest. Maybe it's some kind of ritual greeting.

Half-tusk scrapes the stick along the inner curve of the bark, the fire-plow method! A difficult way to start fires. The iguana generates heat from friction, rubbing the stick faster and faster along the bark to create a groove. The plowing action pushes out particles of wood fibers. They start to smoke. A few more minutes effort would bring flame, but Half-tusk sets them aside and points gnarled fingers to my knife. My turn.

When I take up my rock and knife to make sparks, Half-tusk lets out a sound like, "Ook." I look to where she points. The roots! I forgot to smear my kindling. She waits patiently while I saw off a root and prepare my stick with sap. My showers of sparks catch quickly this time.

As smoke becomes flame, I bob up and down in my nest. "That's it! That's the secret! I know how to make firewood!"

Half-tusk must think I'm crazy. She's been doing this her whole life. Half-tusk points to my knife. She wants to try. I hand over the rock and knife which she examines from every angle. She probably wonders where the magic comes from.

After a few minutes she prepares a stick with sap and mimics the way I held the rock. I wince as she grasps the blade, but she holds the flat just like I did. I would hate to have one of the first encounters between human and iguana result in severed fingers.

Half-tusk swings down the knife handle smashing a finger between knife and rock. "Ook!" she cries out, giving me a sharp look. I'm painfully aware that those teeth could rip out my throat. And she's holding my knife! Half-tusk, however, tries again, adjusting the angle of rock and knife. She strikes the knife gently, producing no sparks, and then harder and harder as she gains confidence. On the sixth or seventh strike, sparks appear, and she soon has the fire lit.

We've crossed the great divide between species. We've given each other something of value. Half-tusk knows how to start a fire more easily, and I know the secret of the forests. It's obvious when I look back, the fruit that nearly smashed Siff's head and ate into the wood, the platforms molded together into a smooth surface, rubbing the wood with sap to change the structure. It's acid. The wood is too dense to burn unless it's soaked in acid. There must be a chemical reaction between the acid and wood, breaking chemical bonds, or puffing out the tissues somehow.

A new generation of trees builds on top of the old generation. To do this the fruit has to break through the bark of an old tree. When fruit drops onto a branch the acid eats through the bark and plants a seed. Iguanas must use acidic fruit to bend branches into a platform. That still doesn't tell me what the platforms are for but with this information the colony's success is assured. If colonists are still alive. Maybe only the Junior Rangers have been killed. It wouldn't be the first mission where I came back alone.

With simple acids the colonists could bend forest branches to make walkways, houses, and farms. Whole cities! They could make more fuel than they could use in a thousand lifetimes. I must get this information back to the Homestead but I'm stuck in the swamp. The Junior Rangers haven't come to my rescue and I can't climb through the mid-level on my own.

While I'm sitting and thinking, Half-tusk reaches out a hand to touch mine. I jump at the touch of freezing scales. The nails are sharp, hard as daggers, but she nods in the direction of the platform. I guess I'll get to eat after all. And warmth! We'll sit in the hothouse and eat alligator eggs until our stomachs burst!

As I pick up my crutches, Half-tusk reaches out to stroke the flat end of the crutch. She looks at the splints on my leg and seems to make the connection. Smart. I wonder if iguanas have medicine.

Junior Rangers find blood on Thuy's skids. Crystal says, "You found them in a pile?"

The mech shakes his head. "They were scattered in the area. I found the watch here."

Anacine says, "No body and no jawbone. Think a gator got him?"

Siff says, [We haven't found his blaster. He might be okay.]

The others look discretely away. If Thuy was alive, he wouldn't have given up his watch or body armor. After a few minutes looking around the cave of roots, Ivan says, "Should we spend night here and start up in morning?"

"What do you mean, thtart up!" Siff shouts. "We're not leaving without Thuy!"

Crystal pats his arm. "We'll look again in the morning. I can't keep my eyes open."

Ivan says, "Too bad we didn't bring metal detector. We might find Thuy's blaster."

Li'l Mike says, "I'll get the detector."

"You'd have to climb to Dragonfly."

"I don't sleep. Do you need anything else?"

The mech doesn't know where Thuy's body is. He found the skids and watch, like he said. If

Junior Rangers had the blaster as well they would give up and climb back to the Homestead. By the time Junior Rangers wake, one way or another, Li'l Mike is going to hand them a blaster.

Thuy's real blaster would be somewhere along the trail or caught up in branches like Thuy's kit. Li'l Mike follows the route that Thuy's watch took through the swamp. He looks for Thuy's body or the blaster. If he can't find either, Li'l Mike will climb to the Dragonfly and take a blaster from the skid locker to pass off as Thuy's. They would all be back on the moon before that blaster was discovered missing. They might trace that to Li'l Mike but it was a small chance.

It takes an hour of backtracking through the swamp to find the egg house. Li'l Mike is surprised to find Thuy climbing higher meter by meter with a knotted vine. Watching silently from the dark, the mech makes plans as Thuy works his way down to the platform. His leg is obviously broken. Iguanas must have built the house, and iguanas must have carried off Thuy's things. Iguanas might finish off Thuy as well, but Li'l Mike can't count on that. He must make sure.

Thuy reaches the platform and ducks through a low doorway. Li'l Mike will snap his neck when he comes out. The mech will retrieve a blaster and metal detector from the Dragonfly, presenting both to the Junior Rangers. Even if Thuy's body is found they'll assume he was killed by iguanas.

The mech is about to move closer when iguanas scramble through the doorway. Very interesting, it looks like iguanas *will* kill him. If so, the mech can bring Junior Rangers back through the swamp to examine the body for themselves.

Focusing sensors on the egg house, Li'l Mike doesn't detect a wiry shape sliding down the trunk overhead. The iguana drops the last meter pulling Li'l Mike off the branch. As they bounce down into the leaves, the mech fights to push away a fang stabbing at his neck.

When Li'l Mike gets his hands up he finds a familiar broken tooth. No wonder it attacked. It's the one Li'l Mike fought before in the canopy. The iguana rips at Li'l Mike's clothes. The mech fights back. It hammers the creature's head with metal fists, but neither can gain advantage.

Very quickly into the fight Li'l Mike decides to run. Thuy won't survive the others. When the mech gets separation, he scampers up a trunk. The iguana doesn't follow. Li'l Mike doesn't wonder why as he climbs for the canopy to complete his deception.

Episode 7 – Society Man

Half-tusk studies my lizard cage as she leads me through the swamp. With giant dodecahedra eyes, iguanas see better than owls or cats, but down this far from the sun there are no photons to see. Creatures generate their own like the alligators or bioluminescent lizards. How do iguanas move through mid-level when there's no light? Air currents? Heat?

Half-tusk pulls back when I hold out the cage. Maybe she's afraid to touch such a fragile object. When we reach the pool underneath the hothouse Half-tusk proves the worth of those talons, climbing a heavy trunk as easily as I would climb a ladder. Platforms keep them safe from alligators, but why build them in the canopy?

I stand in the water wondering how she expects me to climb when a net flies over the side. The knots are as precise as the weave of my cage. Those talons have exact touch as well as strength. I climb the net and stoop to follow Half-tusk through the doorway.

The room is empty of iguanas. Half-tusk checks eggs, tapping and smelling until she finds a ripe one. Half-tusk crouches. I sit on the floor away from the heat of the oven, and she puts the egg between us. My stomach growls in anticipation.

Half-tusk leans close to the egg. Iguanas don't vocalize very often. Sounds must get bounced or absorbed in the forest but Half-tusk purrs to the egg, a deep vibrating sound in her throat. Maybe she's saying grace I think with some impatience. Let's just eat!

Half-tusk taps the egg starting a jagged crack. I reach out to help when the crack expands. The shell falls in two revealing a squirming bundle the size of a bunny. Not an omelet, an alligator dinner we can roast in the oven. I sit back as a creature unfolds. Blue-gray scales, talons, and eyes on top of the head, I watch the birth of a baby iguana. I almost lose my appetite.

I'm not sure why Half-tusk brought me here. She seems to have forgotten me. She has eyes only for the bundle of joy crawling unsteadily across the platform towards the open doorway. "Careful there!"

Half-tusk doesn't budge, and that's a seven-meter fall! The creature's nails click on the wood as it approaches the edge and goes over. After a splash, Half-tusk crawls to the doorway and scans the water. She motions for me to follow. Alligators patrolling the swamp must listen for those splashes. An iguana's life starts in peril. Only the lucky or the strong swimmers make it over the first hurdle.

Half-tusk climbs down to the pool underneath the platform. I climb down the net near the swimming baby iguana. Half-tusk and I stand waist deep in freezing water. By the light of my lizard cage we watch the baby swim to a trunk. It crawls up the side, pauses, and then scoots around the edge. Half-tusk leads me to the other side in time to see the baby's feet disappearing into a hollow cavity. That's why iguanas attacked Terra. Their babies use the hollows to move through the forest.

Our equipment kept disappearing without triggering motion alarms. Maybe full-grown iguanas could use the hollows as well. I wade to the hole and feel around inside. Nothing bites my fingers. Could I climb? Ivan dared me to go inside. Wouldn't he be surprised to see me climbing out of a hollow tree on their platform? *If he's still alive.*

My crutches would never make it up the twisting cavity, but I have to try. A tower begins from a mound of earth. The hole is too small for me and the lizard cage both. I'll be climbing blind until I reach the top. I stick my head into the hollow and then look back at Half-tusk.

In her eyes I can see that this is why she brought me here. She's showing me the ways of the iguana. I hand her the cage, my adaptation to their environment. That is the way of humans. Maybe in the future these cages will decorate iguana platforms like hanging Japanese lanterns. I would like to think so.

When I crouch to squeeze into the hole, Half-tusk's cold hand pulls on my arm. She taps on my splint. Is it too bulky for the passageway? I unwrap the vines letting braces hit the water. When the pressure is released I'm hit by excruciating pain. I bite my lip and bend over to retrieve the braces. Half-tusk watches soberly as I wrap my bones again. Muscles around the break are too sensitive to flap loose. If I had Gravitol I might bear it. For now I'm stuck here a few days at least.

After I finish wrapping, Half-tusk leads me through waist-high water. She scoots along on two legs. Tail swishing below the surface for balance, she holds the lizard cage before her like a lamp in a storm. At large trunks she pauses and listens, talons gripping the roots. As thin as a bowling pin the head swings back to me, and then forward again leading off into the dark.

I hop along on my crutches, Hackman tucked into the splint. Half-tusk pauses when we reach a mud bank leading above the waterline. I know an alligator nest when I smell one. I look for a quick route up the branches. When Half-tusk is sure the nest is empty we hurry through the muddy nest and back down to water.

In thirty minutes we cover about six hundred meters. I have no idea where Half-tusk takes me. I have no attachment to the area where I landed, but if Junior Rangers look for me I don't want to get too far away. Maybe Half-tusk leads me back to the Homestead at the cove. Without the sun I have no idea which direction is north.

I sense them in the swamp around us. Moving through the trunks like ghosts, iguanas pace us. It can't be a trap. Iguanas had me surrounded several times already. I clear my throat nervously. "Half-tusk, is this some kind of test?"

When the iguana looks at me in the light of the lantern, I realize it *is* a test. She leads me like a show pony in front of iguana judges. To what purpose? I lean on my crutches as the procession stops. Iguanas melt out of the trunks, surrounding us, moving closer. Holding the lizard cage high,

Half-tusk calls to them with clicks and grunts. I'm on trial! It looks like the jury is back. By reflex I reach for Hackman, but realistically, I am defenseless against a dozen iguanas as big as guard dogs.

I put weight on my good leg, and drop the crutches as the first attacks. Teeth bared, it flies at me with a leap off powerful hind legs. As I bring up the knife to slash, Half-tusk flies from the side, tackling it into the water with a splash. I expect to see them come up clawing at each others throats.

When they rise again, they face each other to talk. Hissing and ooking, the conversation expands to include the audience. As prosecutor and defense attorney make their cases, I'm amazed at the level of intelligence. Half-tusk passes my lizard cage to the skeptical jury. She grunts and points to my splint. When she makes hacking motions with her arms, I realize she's talking to me. The flint! She wants them to see her pet do a trick!

I dig the rock out of my splint, and shower the air with sparks off Hackman. Iguanas don't kneel down to worship their new god, but neither am I attacked. Iguanas melt back into the swamp heading back the way we came. Half-tusk turns me with a hand on my crutch, leading us after her tribe. I passed an initial screening. Maybe an interview with the Big Boss still looms.

What was it that changed the iguana's minds? I have no doubt they would have killed me if Half-tusk hadn't intervened. Is this still about the baby iguana I was going to eat? Maybe Half-tusk was trying to sneak me out earlier in their baby highway. She has been both my tormentor, stealing a light pole to lead me down here, and my protector. She's a reptilian angel of the underworld. I have no choice but to accept her guidance now.

As the swampland rises I believe we've turned off from the path we were on before. Root balls grow close, producing a winding wooden staircase. I can't see past the dim glow of the lizard cage so I don't see the other iguanas until we climb up through a trapdoor cut in the wood.

The door slams down behind leaving me on a branch with about thirty iguanas of all sizes. Half-tusk locks the door in place with a sliding brace like a deadbolt in a medieval castle. I'm in favor of sealing out alligators, but it adds pressure to the whole meeting-the-family.

After an initial inspection young iguanas crawl off to spots on the horizontal branches that make up some kind of picnic ground. It's not a platform but the area is lived-in with numerous glow lizards lying about. Nets, ropes, and hammocks hang from smaller branches. They remind me of the tents and rugs of nomadic desert tribes. Are iguanas territorial or a nomadic species, moving on when the local food supply runs low? It's hard to think of a bunch of giant lizards as having a strategy. Maybe they migrate by instinct or from environmental clues.

Water is supplied in animal skins or gourds. When iguanas carry around hanging baskets of food my stomach lets out a loud growl. I glance to see if Half-tusk notices but she's busy pulling out melons, whole fish, small chunks of meat, and green leaves that must have come from the surface.

Like a good hostess, Half-tusk picks out portions for me as well, setting them on the branch. It's not exactly sanitary, but I gratefully eat everything but the leaves. A lot of the kids aren't touching their greens either. When iguanas want more light they grab one of the scattered bioluminescent lizards, and set them on a nearby branch. With a leaf to munch on, the lizards stay in place.

A few of the kids finish early. They chase each other around the walls and crawl upside down along overhead branches. Older iguanas waddle over to hammocks rolling heavily inside to sleep off the meal. Two things strike me about the domestic scene. Most animals will eat whenever they come across food. They don't store it in baskets, or carry it great distances to share, and gathering to eat is a social activity. It promotes unity in the group and conformity to social norms. It also requires a huge increase in intelligence to understand one's place in that society, reading intentions in others, and scheming to move up in the hierarchy.

The second thing that strikes me is that this social group of iguanas is letting me eat with them. An hour ago they were going to kill me. Now one of them waddles by to refill my water gourd? It doesn't make sense. If I was a threat, why the change?

Maybe they weren't really mad at me in the first place. When I was about to eat their baby, they just knocked me off the platform. They didn't attack. I still have a lot to learn about iguanas, but hopefully I'll never have to. As soon as my leg can stand the stress, I plan to climb out through the hollow trunks.

After dinner, iguanas hang by their tails or wedge themselves into nooks to sleep. I follow their example, stretching out of a flat branch. I feel comfortable for the first time since my long fall. With all these bodies around me I have a powerful sense of security. That's another benefit of living within a society. Attack one, and you attack us all.

I don't know what signals iguanas get inside the pitch black swamp but hours later they start stretching and yawning. Maybe it's a slight increase in temperature from Klondike's rising sun. Maybe the group moves by consensus. One thing I'm sure of, they don't have to hurry off to work.

Water skins are passed around again. We have a light meal of fish and acid melon. My leg feels better when I stand up. With a little uninterrupted rest the bone's sintered ends got a chance to fuse. As larger iguanas pull long poles from the walls I sense excitement in the troop. Half-tusk argues with the others again. I check for the knife in my splint. I assume that the larger iguanas are males. They gather in front of me with pointed spears. At least I got a last meal and a good nap.

Half-tusk doesn't put up a fight when they lead me to the trapdoor. She follows us down through the winding staircase. Our group of males and Half-tusk head off through the swamp. After we've gone a hundred meters, they pull logs from the trees. As they splash into the water, I say out loud, "Canoes!"

Half-tusk looks on disapprovingly, and iguanas scramble over the sides into the flat-bottomed boats. As I wonder what I'm doing here, a boat bumps into me from behind. Half-tusk grunts, "Ook", and takes my crutches. I lift my splint gingerly over the side. I bite my lip with the banging it's taking, but iguanas are watching again. Is this another test? I wish I knew what the rules are so I could raise my performance.

A male in the back of the canoe hands me a paddle. Half-tusk gets another and scrambles into the front spot. The paddle has a flat end like my crutch. No wonder Half-tusk took an interest. Tool-users always want to know what the next guy is using.

The procession of canoes moves off in a line, iguanas stroking in rhythm, three to a boat. I guess the toy we found earlier on the platform really was a model canoe. That implies symbolism and artistic creativity. What's next, technology?

I wouldn't think a swamp would be an easy place to navigate, but our canoes pick up speed. Dodging in and out of trunks we sometimes bump over high roots in the water. It almost feels like a race as the canoes split wide so that we're four across. "Stoke! Stroke!" I say to my teammates until I realize we're not racing, but hunting. Iguanas drum their paddles against the sides to make a steady booming wall of sound. We're driving prey!

The spears at the iguana's sides must be for alligators but I've seen how strong the gators are.

I'm not sure that an iguana with a spear is an even fight. Our boat is the second from the right. As the water shallows, the boat to the far right edges closer until our bows nearly touch. The iguana behind me turns us further into deeper water. We seem to be scraping the edge of an island of mud. We paddle for about five hundred meters until a cry goes up. An alligator has been sighted.

We dig in with paddles, iguanas hooting directions until the long, white body is zigzagging around roots ahead of us. The canoes to our left shoot forward while our two on the right stay behind.

The alligator climbs roots with frightening quickness until it's perched on a hillock over our heads. As we surround it, paddles are exchanged for spears. I would think the alligator's advantage would be in the water, and then it dives off the roots, spilling canoes into the water with a crash.

Iguanas dumped in the water swim fast to the roots while spears from the boats jab at the alligator, mine along with them. Half-tusk and the male behind me stand for more power. With my broken leg I have to sit. I'm still getting in a few good sticks when the alligator rolls, slapping our boat with its tail and knocking Half-tusk and the male into the water. I'm thrown to the floor on my face, losing my spear. I'm up in a flash with Hackman unleashed.

Iguanas dive from the roots overhead with teeth and talons. The water churns with iguanas latched onto the alligator like ants bringing down a grasshopper. I'm the only one still in a boat. I get the feeling this is not where I'm supposed to be.

I see an opening at the throat so I give a yell and spring from the boat. My leg's on fire but I hook my good leg around a flipper, stabbing repeatedly at the tough, scaly skin. Hot blood mixes with cold water pouring down my chest. The alligator thrashes and rolls. Teeth never get close. I keep stabbing as I'm turned under the water, but I sense that life has gone out of the beast.

Nearly crying out from the pain I sink to the bottom and move slowly sideways. When I rise next to the dead alligator, iguanas stand to the sides watching. They don't say anything but I sense I passed another test. I'm glad I didn't wait in the boat. When in doubt, dive in.

Canoes are emptied of water and re-floated. Spears are retrieved and the alligator tied by the tail to my canoe. My reward for killing the beast is the honor of towing it home. Iguanas climb into the boats. Before we put paddles to water, Half-tusk cries out, pointing to the canoe in front of us.

The iguana in back hides a crooked right arm. I thought I saw him pinned against the root trunk, but I have a hard time telling them apart. The injured iguana holds the paddle bravely with the other arm but he's clearly in pain and terrified. The middle one stands and turns around. He takes the paddle away from "Lefty" and they exchange places. Lefty gets to ride home.

The hunting party seems more subdued as we paddle slowly in single file. We haven't gone a hundred meters when we approach iguanas hanging silently from branches above the swamp. They're all big males, and I don't think they're from Half-tusk's tribe.

Canoes slow as iguanas let go of paddles and put talons to spears. The newcomers look over the dead alligator. I guess we were hunting in their territory. One of our iguanas dives over the side. When he stands waist-high in the water his partner hands him a spear. A large iguana from the new tribe drops from a branch and comes up with a rock lashed onto the end of a stick like a mace. The iguanas stand eye to eye in the water. Our side is outnumbered but it looks like only the two will fight.

Iguanas hiss back and forth to each other, gesturing at their warriors, their superior weapons, or the forest itself. The newcomer shakes his mace, ours pounds the butt of his spear on bedrock. Our leader points to me. The other chief points to me and then suddenly their whole tribe looks at me. I'm being given up for ransom! I hope my new tribe likes showers of sparks.

It's over as soon as it starts. The chief climbs back into his canoe and we paddle away. I guess that answers the question about nomadic versus territorial. I wonder why we get to take their alligator home?

The body is left in the water outside our winding staircase. I limp up with my crutches through the trapdoor, happy to be home again. I lay on the floor exhausted and unwrap my splint. I know I tore loose the bones again.

As hunters put their spears away, Lefty stands alone in the middle of the room with his broken arm. He turns around to show the family, grunting and clicking quietly. He must be explaining why he won't be doing any chores, I think, when a hunter runs at him with a spear pointed towards his throat.

"Look out!" I shout, lunging for the iguana. My hand trips up his foot, sending the big male sprawling over the uneven log floor.

The tribe is stunned, glaring at me, and none is angrier than Lefty. As the spearman climbs to his feet, Half-tusk scrambles between us. She rises and speaks, addressing the whole group as well as the big male. As she points to my leg and then Lefty's arm I figure it out. How stupid could I be? Iguanas are arboreal creatures. They need all four limbs to live. Lefty and I only have three.

They weren't killing us out of anger but as a mercy. We'd be unable to survive on our own, and our injuries would weaken the tribe. Iguanas never invented medicines. They just kill anyone who gets hurt. No hard feelings but that's the way nature works here.

But why is Half-tusk different? Why did she save me? Is it because of her own dental infirmity that she can see worth in others? Maybe that's why she brought me back to the tribe, to show them a different way. Lefty breathes hard in the middle of the room. If I try to splint his arm, it looks like he'll rip *my* throat out. Still, I have to try.

I rise on crutches to approach him side-by-side with Half-tusk. She's going to help! While

Half-tusk grunts calming words, I examine the bone through the skin. It's a simple break like mine. If I can set it and wrap it tight with vines it should mend fine. Stay off it for a few weeks and he should be good as new, but how can I get him to understand?

I tear up most of the rest of my tattered jumpsuit to make a bandage for underneath the vines. If I'm here much longer I'll be down to a loincloth. Not that iguanas would care if I lost even that. While the whole tribe watches I have Lefty lie on his back on the ground. I show Half-tusk how to hold him and then give a smooth, hard pull to straighten the humerus. Lefty squirms and howls but doesn't bite. After the bones click into place I move fast to wrap them tight with cloth. It was a cleaner break than mine, I think sourly.

Over the cloth I wrap vines and immobilize the arm around his body. When I'm done and help Lefty sit up, he stares at the arm in wonder. He looks around at the other iguanas, still not quite believing his strange fortunes. We have dinner again and turn in to sleep.

When I catch Lefty chewing at the vines at his shoulder, I slap his skinny head and say, "No!" Lefty crawls off on three legs to sulk but he leaves the vines alone.

After Junior Rangers wake inside their cave of roots, Li'l Mike shows them a blaster. "I found it up top, close to where Thuy fell. He never had it in the swamp."

Crystal shakes her head. "No light, no heat, no skids."

[No body,] Siff says angrily. [You aren't thinking about giving up, are you?]

"We said we'll look again, Siff."

[You say it like there's a time limit.]

Anacine says, "Eat something, nothing has been decided. I assume you'll want to be back for the return trip to the moon?"

Still muttering, Siff digs through his kit for a bricko. After Junior Rangers eat and pack their kits, Ivan turns to Siff, "Where to?"

[Along the trail from where Thuy fell. We got the metal detector. Even if he's dead, Hackman will be clutched in Thuy's cold fingers.]

Junior Rangers don't give up as the mech predicted. There's a small chance that Thuy survived at the egg house. If Junior Rangers find him, the mech will be back to square one. They will probably never leave the Dragonfly again.

There are three ways to complete his mission, run ahead to make sure Thuy's dead, kill a different Junior Ranger along the trail, or lead the Junior Rangers away from Thuy's camp. Data registers churn through models until Li'l Mike has the optimal solution. He'll lead Junior Rangers through an area infested with alligators. While they fight for their lives, Li'l Mike will slip away to finish off Thuy. The mech says, "I'll scout ahead for an easy route."

Anacine says, "With a few dozen mechs along, building a colony would be a snap."

"That's the idea," Li'l Mike sniffs, climbing a root with pins on hands and feet.

Humans will need at least an hour to reach Thuy's original landing spot eight hundred meters away. As he scouts the terrain, Li'l Mike will scamper back and forth several times that distance. Grunting with effort on the first difficult climb, Ivan codes, [Don't get too far ahead, Li'l Mike.]

So they won't get suspicious, Li'l Mike calculates that he can take the Junior Rangers only a few hundred meters to either side of the straight-line path. Patrolling throughout the day, alligators don't sit in one spot. Getting alligators and humans to meet will be a challenge, until he finds a nest with juveniles and a mother alligator nearby. The mech returns to find the humans wading thigh-deep through a pool. "This way. Not far now."

Junior Rangers turn to Li'l Mike's globe adjusting their route. If they had been hiking alone they would keep fingers on triggers. Trusting their guide, Junior Rangers keep blasters slung across their backs. If Li'l Mike had been capable of guilt, his programs would be conflicted. Keeping suspicion from himself, Li'l Mike says, "I saw an alligator off to the right. Keep your eyes open. I'm going to look ahead for a clear path."

Crystal says, "Do you think we should climb?"

"You should climb back to the Dragonfly. Why risk your necks when I can look for Thuy myself?"

The mech studies facial expressions. Ivan and Crystal seem ready to go back. Siff and

Anacine want to press ahead. After alligators attack, Li'l Mike will count votes again. "I'll scout ahead."

When Junior Rangers can't miss the nest, Li'l Mike scrambles off to check on Thuy. Siff has the metal detector but the mech's infrared eyes are better. Even if Thuy died, his body would generate heat. Bacteria would live for some days consuming whatever was left worth eating.

Li'l Mike turns off his globe, and steals silently through the forest. The egg house blazes like a sun in the mech's eyes. Thuy's body could be inside where iguanas attacked. Li'l Mike climbs the platform to find the room empty. Under normal conditions, Li'l Mike would report the egg house. Its importance is obvious, but until Li'l Mike finds the body he doesn't want Junior Rangers hanging around.

The mech climbs down to search the swamp. Thuy's nest of sticks is empty. An overhanging branch is hacked to pieces. Thuy must have had a knife at one point. Li'l Mike searches the area until he hears blaster fire. If Thuy is still alive he might head in that direction. The mech starts back to collect data and rethink the problem. If Li'l Mike can't verify that Thuy is dead, he'll have to pick another one to kill.

On my third day as a member of Half-tusk's tribe, iguanas prepare to move. I check Lefty's wrap to make sure it's still in place. I wonder how I'm going to keep him from leaving camp with the others but it looks like everyone's going. If the tribe goes higher into the trunks I'll be left behind as well.

Half-tusk drags a net over, holding it to my shoulders for size. As she hands it to me, Half-tusk's grunting seems overburdened. Well, I didn't ask to go along! During the preparations, Lefty sits alone. His situation is unique, and Lefty doesn't know what to expect any better than I do. I drag my net to him indicating that we could both fit inside. Lefty looks to Half-tusk, grunting, "Ook?"

Without committing herself, Half-tusk crawls off to confer with others. While we sit next to each other waiting for an answer, Lefty reaches out a claw to rest on my knee. Most of the bags and nets around camp are carried through the trapdoor, but spears are left behind. So it's not a hunting party. Maybe we're going to restock the pantry. After the women and children leave, it's our turn. Half-tusk includes both Lefty and me in a sweep of her arm.

Lefty makes sure he's seen helping with the net. I wonder about a society that kills off its crippled. Why not just run them off to die on their own? Or better yet, let them contribute what they can. Lefty could still climb and gather things with three limbs, just not as fast. Are they afraid he'll take more energy out of the tribe than he contributes? Societies on the edge are always more brutal. It tells me that iguanas have to fight to survive.

Outside camp the whole tribe climbs trunks with nets or bags hanging off their backs in slings. Limbs are left free to climb. Lefty and I stand on the net with the edges held to our shoulders. Larger iguanas run ropes through the net and put loops around their necks. I don't see how iguanas can coordinate their movements past sticks and branches up through the forest but we're swept off our feet, dangling above water as the team climbs.

It's not a smooth rise. We rock back and forth like a pendulum. I can only imagine the strain on climbers. Maybe I shouldn't have invited Lefty into the net. We get banged around quite a bit. For Lefty it definitely beats a spear in the throat, and for me, I'm moving closer to our treetop platform. If we're going all the way to the top for green leaves we'll be within jawbone range.

Another team climbs steadily below us. Shackled with harnesses I can't see what they're lifting until they pull even. The white body of the alligator lies curled like a snake at the bottom of a net. Where are we going? They could have butchered the alligator below and carried it up in chunks. It reminds me of the sometimes incomprehensibility of different cultures. It's best not to try to draw parallels to your own. Admire each culture for its strengths. Any society that evolves and survives has lessons to teach.

The alligator team pulls even with ours. I'm not sure how they do it, but iguanas weave in and out of our ropes to go past. The alligator net swings within a meter of our own, and the swampy carcass goes by. Our net is the last in line. Once I'm over the excitement of the passing alligator I settle myself for a boring kilometer-long climb to the top.

At this rate I calculate it'll take about four hours if we don't stop for breaks.

The rocking of the net lulls me to sleep. I wake to a howling and screeching in the pitch-black forest overhead. Lefty wakes too with fear in his eyes. He wraps arms tighter around me, talons pressing into my back. "Easy there," I whisper, as our net continues its slow rise.

Whatever the commotion, it doesn't hurry our team. We climb slowly to a platform. As we rise above the floor, over a hundred iguanas mill around, climbing on branches and screeching at each other. Lizard-lanterns as complicated as my own light the floor space and branches above. It feels like a circus tent in a giant bubble of light. Reptile acts proceed in all three rings at once.

On the platform a group of large iguanas stands around the alligator carcass. This is the group that confronted us below in the swamp! This is a peace conference or negotiation of some sort between tribes.

Our team climbs above the platform and onto an overhanging branch to bring the net over the platform. We're dropped roughly to the deck. Our porters may not have been so happy about their assignment. My leg is okay and Lefty appears to be unhurt as he stands. Half-tusk untangles the net while newcomers gather around to watch.

Half-tusk seems agitated, hissing and snapping as she leads us away from the group. Newcomer iguanas follow us slowly. I don't see any weapons but I have a distinct sense of danger.

As we head towards our iguanas, a newcomer jumps out of the pack to pull on Lefty's good arm. They're trying to separate him! I whip out my knife, swinging it at the newcomer mob. They would kill Lefty for the same reason his own tribe would! Injury is not tolerated among iguanas.

Half-tusk and Lefty break into a gallop as I swing Hackman at the crowd. I guess I'm odd enough to distract the newcomers, but they keep clicking and grunting, pointing to Lefty who looks terrified. When it looks like newcomers will claim Lefty for a sacrifice, Lefty's family intercedes to save him.

Even though they were about to kill him themselves, Lefty's tribe takes offense at someone else doing it. I take that as a good sign. Maybe this will be the start of iguana medicine, and me the first doctor.

After social mixing between tribes, the alligator is butchered. Food is brought out of bags and shared. We scoop drinking water from the long pool in the middle of the platform. There is extended family from both sides as some of their iguanas sit in groups of ours and some of our iguanas sit with them, touching and caressing. I wonder if there's a dowry system or trading of eligible young iguanas to strengthen genetic lines. It certainly seems their tribe is more prosperous.

After the meal, nets and bags are cleared to the sides or to branches above the platform. Women, children, and many of the males climb into the overhead branches. I look to Half-tusk for some clue. It looks like there's more to this meeting than a sharing of the disputed alligator.

Half-tusk rises from her bloated belly, and leads Lefty and I to a net hanging from a branch. Some of the children and older iguanas used this for a less strenuous climb to the bleachers. After we're seated among the lanterns, males from each tribe are left on the platform. Is it to be combat? Square dancing? A football game?

They certainly look like combatants standing in two lines, hooting and puffing chests. I wish I had my watch camera to record for the Rangers. I almost forgot! I don't know how far we climbed while I slept. [Siff? Anacine? Anyone there?] No answer. After what... three... four days, I conclude they must be dead. All the more reason to fit into iguana society.

Iguana teams rise on hind legs. Feinting as if to charge they hold talons before them like boxers. The hooting noise grows in intensity. At some predetermined signal, both sides throw down their hands. Small objects scatter across the platform like gravel. Contestants freeze and look around the platform. All the tension is gone. Iguanas from both sides hoot laughter, pointing at dots around their feet. I squint in the dim light, catching glints of red or blue. "Marbles?"

Half-tusk spares me a quick glance but is drawn back to the action. Lefty doesn't even look at me. Members from the teams pair off, stepping carefully to the sides of the platform. Both contestants and audience study the map laid out before them with armies of red and blue marbles laying in proximity.

I think the pool in the middle of the platform will hinder play but toy canoes sit at the pool's edge. They're canoes for marbles! No doubt they're used in the game to float in behind a competitor.

When it's time for the first pair, teams gather around their champions to discuss strategy. Both sides are animated as advice is screamed from the rafters. One of my iguanas, I think, crouches down on all fours to line a marble in his sights. With a flick of his talon the red marble rolls across the warped platform to click into a blue marble. The crowd goes wild. It *is* one of my iguanas by Lefty and Half-tusk's reactions. I cheer just as hard as the blue marble is removed.

It's the other team's turn. The iguana for blue team eyes a marble less than a meter away. When he hurries his shot and flicks the blue stone wide, both sides of iguanas howl derisively. I'm glad I'm not down there in that pressure cooker. The next pair comes out, studying a different region of the platform. I gather there are complicated strategies for defending territories.

After a dozen moves, a boat is brought into play. If a marble rolls into the water, it's forfeit. If it stops within one claws-width of the edge the marble is put on a boat and flicked across the pool where the marble is removed and placed on land. Counting the number of marbles on the platform I would guess the game lasts several hours but it never gets boring. At first I think blue team will easily overwhelm red. After a lucky streak, red comes back, launching a bold counterattack into blue's stronghold and taking out three blues with a single flick.

After a player shoots, he sometimes climbs into the branches to be congratulated or comforted by his family. A lot of food is consumed during the match and when a marble rolls over the side, youths from both tribes goes screaming down into the dark to try and catch it. Lefty looks on jealously. When I catch him chewing at his bandages, I slap his head in rebuke.

All too soon the game winds down with blue rebounding and seemingly invincible with a sixteen to three advantage. For a long time red plays defense, rolling long distances to stay out of blue's reach, but one-by-one they're cornered and taken out.

After the last red marble is nicked, both teams gather to congratulate each other, recalling amazing shots made and easy shots missed. The families of both tribes climb down out of the branches. Bags of a fermented drink are passed around. As iguanas slowly get drunk, I wonder what the marble contest proves. Is it purely a social gathering or do they set boundaries or exchange property based on the results?

Thousands of years ago tribes of iguanas probably battled over food, mates, and territory before developing the elaborate marble game. Maybe a winning team proves its mastery of tactics. Platforms are like sport's stadiums on Earth, cathedrals of symbolic violence that let us safely vent biological instincts to kill.

As iguanas fall asleep in each others arms, Half-tusk pulls me to the edge of the platform. She looks around to make sure no one's watching, and then pushes me towards a hole in the trunk. This is it! Maybe I'm close enough to the top! The hole is small. I'll have to leave behind objects I've collected: lizard cage, crutches, splint.

Sensing that this trip will either make or break me, I give Half-tusk my knife and flint. If I make it to the treetop platform I'll have all kinds of tools. If I don't, I'll be rotting in a hollow tree trunk somewhere along the way. Half-tusk expertly strikes the rock and knife together producing a shower of sparks in farewell.

I now understand the iguana's fascination with light and fire. They are born in cold dark swamps before moving up to the canopy. In the earliest days of the planet, sunlight would be close to the top. Over tens of thousands of years as the canopy grew further and further away the journey became more dangerous. The swamp became colder. Alligators probably snatched babies before iguanas learned to build platforms and burn hollows into giant trunks.

Days earlier that baby jumped from the platform. I'm not sure why iguana babies aren't allowed direct access to the system of hollow trunks. Why the pool? Why the gauntlet of alligators? Is it a test to weed out weaker members of the species? Maybe weaker iguanas create a burden on the troop, like the injured. Maybe some die or get lost on the long climb.

Nature is the great sorter, constantly shuffling winners and losers: individuals, species, whole planets. Like the Junior Rangers, I guess. Will I be sorted into the winner's circle one more time while my fellow Junior Rangers suffered some calamity above?

Iguanas use fire to keep their eggs warm. I wouldn't be surprised to see fires on platforms higher up as well, the mark of their civilization. That the iguanas are intelligent and civilized I have no doubt. Now if I can only make it back and tell whoever's left to care. I squirm into the hollow of the tree, pressing my back to the wall. Dangling my broken leg, my good leg pushes on the rough wall scooting me up a centimeter at a time. No place for the claustrophobic.

It's pitch black inside the hollow corridor, but it feels warmer inside the heart of a living tree. On Earth I'd worry about spider webs, bats, and insects. The iguana highway is clear so far. Every twenty meters or so the trunk opens to the outside. I pause at these intersections to breathe fresh air and look for signs of light. I'm still too far down.

After an hour I halt to regain some strength. In a curving section of hollow, I curl up and fall asleep. Iguanas will just have to pinch me if they want to get by. I wake instead when a stream of water falls down through the corridor like a waterfall. It must be raining up top. Maybe these hollows catch water and move them to storage reservoirs on the platforms. I'll have to ask Terra about that.

The thought of home gets me moving. I climb all morning? Afternoon? In complete darkness time has no meaning. At one intersection I find a platform. I crawl out and feel around the edges to verify the discovery but it's pitch black. I return nervously to the safety of the trunk.

I wonder where that baby iguana ended up. It could be in the canopy by now or have crawled out at any one of the numerous intersections. I hope it finds its family okay. Maybe it should worry about me. I move automatically, step, push up, brace... step, push up, brace... My mind wanders. When I see light above my head I assume it's another of my many waking dreams. Siff yells, "Ivan! Get out here with a thovel now!"

I come slowly to my senses, but I don't call out at once. I feel like I'm a part of Klondike-2 now. I climb quietly to the opening and look out over a growing farm. Humans covered the platform with dirt and neat rows of green shoots. The newly fixed Dragonfly sits nearby with a pile of equipment stacked around it. How easy it would be to scramble out, grab a box, and disappear back into the tree. No, I'm a Junior Ranger. That's my stuff, isn't it?

And then it hits me, why aren't the Junior Rangers searching for me! It's like they've just moved on with their lives. I growl a deep iguana sound in my throat. As I climb out of the hollow, Li'l Mike stands next to Siff on the platform. It almost looks like Li'l Mike is going to push Siff over the edge. That can't be right. I shout, "Siff! Behind you!"

Episode 8 – The Assassin

Siff jumps and nearly falls over the edge. He spins with the shovel, glancing at Li'l Mike and then at me. As I crawl onto the platform Anacine comes running from the Dragonfly's hatch with her blaster.

The mech looks as shocked as my friends. Nearly naked, bruised purple, and covered with mud, they don't even know it's me. I wipe dirt from my eyes and laugh. Rolling on the platform, I hold my broken leg and laugh.

Siff stands over me with a shovel. [Thuy?]

I guess it was a shock when I fell out of the tree, but I tire of my friends staring at me like I'm a ghost. [I can't believe it!] Siff says. [I just can't believe it!]

Anacine says, "We thought you were dead, mate!"

"It's only been four days! I wouldn't give up looking for you after four days!"

"We found your kit and skids. They were all bloody."

I stand up, balancing on one leg, "That reminds me, broken leg. Could you help me to my bunk?"

Ivan groans, "Not in my nice clean ship. We'll hose you off outside."

I guess where upholstery is concerned, being a hero doesn't count for much. As Anacine pours

169

buckets of cold water over my head, I say, "Even if you found my stuff you could have looked for a body!"

Crystal says, "We were down two days, mon. Li'l Mike found your blaster in a tree, we were attacked by swamp alligators. We thought you were eaten."

"At least you tried," I say sarcastically.

Siff says, [How did you get up anyway?]

"With a little help from a friend."

While Anacine puts my leg into a proper cast, I tell the Junior Rangers about my adventure. They look skeptical, and I see more than a few glances at my head to check for dents. "It's all true. Bring me a fruit!"

I smash open a melon with a stick, and repeatedly whack it to soak in the juices. I thrust it at Crystal's face. "Check it."

"What am I supposed to see?"

"It's melting. That's how iguanas weave these platforms together."

Siff scratches his head. [Hey buddy, do you see it melting?]

The stick looks the same. "Maybe it takes awhile." I whirl to Ivan. "Light it. This is how they make the stadiums for playing marbles!"

Ivan raises his hands, "Take it easy, Thuy. You had long fall, maybe hit your head several times?"

"As a matter of fact I did hit my head, and I'd be dead if I let you laugh me out of my skids. That doesn't change what I've seen. Anacine?"

Anacine brings a lighter from her kit and holds it under the stick. When the flame catches, I watch smugly as faces turn from worry to amazement. Crystal says, "Go, Thuy! How did you do that?"

"I told you, acid. This whole forest can be turned into fuel. The colonists can build platforms, roads, and farms wherever they want."

Ivan says, "I'm calling emergency meeting with Rangers and colonists. They'll be happy to finally get out of swamp. They were talking about setting up floating rafts on ocean."

"And the iguanas are highly intelligent. Whatever we don't know about this world they can show us."

"Intelligent iguanas?"

"They'll trade, I'm sure of it. It's a tough world, but we can trade flashlights or matches. They'll bring all the food we want, or patrol the swamp for alligators, or help build cities in the trees. They aren't thieves, just curious."

"That's project for future. Rangers have only few days left."

Crystal says, "I agree, mon. We've earned a rest. As usual, a Junior Ranger saves the day."

"I thought I was the last survivor of the Junior Rangers. When you didn't come, I assumed you all were dead."

Siff says, [We're really sorry, Thuy. We gave up on you. We shouldn't have.]

I wave a hand magnanimously. "You don't have as much experience. A battle's not fought in the war room."

[Huh? Now I *know* that doesn't mean anything.]

I roll my eyes. "Isn't it obvious? You gave up the search because of the odds against me, not the bloody skids. You didn't take into account my will to survive."

Crystal pats my cast. "We'll never make that mistake again. Next time we'll make sure you're dead, and it isn't as bad as you make it sound. We came back up after the alligators attacked. Li'l Mike went down several times looking for your body."

I look out the window as Li'l Mike tends the soil with a hoe. Little things click into place. "Where was Li'l Mike when the alligators attacked?"

"He was with us. I mean he was scouting a route through the swamp."

"Li'l Mike was right above the iguanas before I fell."

"So?"

"As I was climbing out of the hollow, Li'l Mike was standing right next to Siff at the edge. It seemed... Well, you may think I'm crazy, but it seemed like Li'l Mike was about to push Siff over."

Ivan says, "Li'l Mike showed us blaster that he said was yours. I knew it was from Dragonfly locker, but I couldn't be sure you didn't take it out yourself."

"I didn't," I say, staring coldly out the window.

Anacine says, "Li'l Mike was supposed to scout a path through the swamp but we walked right into an alligator nest. We thought we just made a wrong turn, but we weren't suspicious enough to go back and check."

"You didn't make a wrong turn. Li'l Mike is trying to kill us."

Ivan says, "Li'l Mike doesn't operate without orders. It would be Doc Blaitel telling him to. Maybe Ranger administration."

Anacine says, "No one has to kill us. We could be dismissed with a word."

Siff says, [Maybe it's not Blaitel. Maybe one of the Rangers programmed Li'l Mike.]

"Blaitel did say there were both pro and anti Junior Ranger factions. Maybe Nofree didn't like having the mech taken away."

Crystal says, "We still got the original programs we took from Li'l Mike as Segundo. We can compare them to the current Li'l Mike to see if anything changed."

I say, "Blaitel will detect it if we mess around inside Li'l Mike's programs, and if Blaitel *is* trying to kill us, we shouldn't tip him off."

Ivan says, "This could all be coincidence, but we have to know if mech is killer."

Anacine says, "Let's put Siff and Li'l Mike out there alone. If Li'l Mike pushes him off we got our mech."

[Hey!]

"You'll have safety cable on leg."

[What if Li'l Mike cracks me over the head with a pick?]

"We'll have hidden camera just in case. Don't be baby."

Siff grumbles, [Alright, after dinner you keep Li'l Mike in here while I set up. Crystal, you got that cable? I'll run it out through my pant's leg.]

With Li'l Mike in attendance, it's difficult making light dinner conversation. Junior Rangers fill me in on the colony's progress. Farms have been started on platforms scattered over eight square kilometers. They deal with slippery iguanas in different ways, from tasers to electric wiring to bribes. So far none have resorted to poisoning. I think iguanas might be too smart for that anyway.

Li'l Mike seems distracted, not joining the conversation except at one point asking confirmation of the number of days left on Klondike-2. We ask after Doc Blaitel's health. Li'l Mike says he's not been in contact since the mission started. Maybe Doc Blaitel doesn't want suspicion on himself when Junior Rangers wake up with their throats cut. After dinner I stretch and yawn. "Well I'm just glad to have my soft warm bed. I'm going to sleep."

Ivan says, "Da. We should all go to bed early and head back to Homestead in morning."

Siff says, [You go ahead. I want to finish up that row of strawberries.]

"Be careful, comrade. On that side of platform it's long fall to next branch."

When the mech rises to follow Siff, Crystal says, "Li'l Mike, could you help me with some loose wiring on this leg?"

Li'l Mike glances at Siff heading out the hatch before he begrudgingly turns to help Crystal. Now that we know what to look for, we read ill intent in the mech's every gesture. Could it be a complete misunderstanding? That would certainly make our lives less complicated. It's never nice to be targeted by a killer. It's especially bad if it's your psychiatrist.

Ivan, Anacine, and I are already in bed by the time Li'l Mike finishes soldering the wire cable. Crystal says, "Thanks, Li'l Mike. I guess I'll turn in too."

The mech puts away his soldering iron. "This is work you could have done yourself."

Crystal looks at us and shrugs. "My camera eye is acting up?"

"I hope you don't want me to look at that as well," Li'l Mike says dryly.

Li'l Mike walks outside, and firmly shuts the hatch. Ivan says, "Put on pogs. Dragonfly's nose camera is recording."

Anacine says, "Can Li'l Mike see that?"

"Nyet. Status registers show it's off. How long do you think we have to wait?"

A chill runs down my spine as Li'l Mike picks up a shovel and heads for the strawberries. Not too long I'd wager. As the mech pauses and looks back, I say, "Lay still. Li'l Mike's infrared eyes can tell if we're in our bunks."

We don't code to Siff. Li'l Mike listens over the jawbone. All we can do is watch as Siff and Li'l Mike tend the garden. With a cable running from his leg Siff can't move too far away. He turns his back several times looking over the edge but Li'l Mike doesn't move. Anacine says, "Maybe we got it all wrong."

"Just wait," I say, but I have doubts.

After ten minutes working the same five plants, Siff yawns. [Well, a few more minutes and I'm done.]

The mech nods but says nothing. Li'l Mike turns on a watering hose, spraying mud off the platform and over the edge into space. It happens so fast we can't believe our eyes. One second Siff is bending down to pick up his rake, and the next he's simply gone. Standing nearby with the watering hose, Li'l Mike doesn't seem to move.

Siff shouts in our heads, [Get him! Get him! Get him!]

Anacine says, "Did Siff jump? Ivan, play that back."

Crystal and Anacine race outside to get Siff hanging upside down below the platform. Li'l Mike continues to water, seemingly caught in confusion. Ivan takes a blaster from below his seat. "Thuy, lock Dragonfly behind us," he says grimly.

With a broken leg I'm left behind while the action occurs outside. They pull Siff back to the platform. Ivan holds the blaster on Li'l Mike who calmly shuts off the water. I replay the tape in slow motion, watching Li'l Mike loop the hose in half. In a flicking motion that looks like he's pulling the hose from an obstruction, the fold whips out to knock Siff off the platform. He'll have a nasty welt on his butt. [No question,] I code. [Li'l Mike whacked Siff on purpose.]

Ivan gestures with the blaster. "Alright, get inside. One false move and I blow head off."

The mech doesn't plead for his life. Other than following orders, Li'l Mike probably doesn't care one way or the other. When we have him surrounded in the hold of the Dragonfly, it could be any normal mission briefing. Crystal says, "Okay, Li'l Mike. Why did you try to kill Siff?"

The mech rejects several models based on lies. Junior Rangers would never trust him again, and Li'l Mike would never get his chance to kill. Getting caught doesn't change his orders. The mech still plots to replace one of the Junior Rangers. Only the truth might still give him a chance. Li'l Mike morphs his features to the verge of tears. "Doc Blaitel programmed me to kill one of you. I couldn't disobey."

We believe the statement instantly, but we are stunned even so. Anacine says, "Whatever for, mate?"

"I'm to replace one of you as a Junior Ranger."

I say, "Doc Blaitel said these mechs were being developed to help colonists. He didn't tell us they were meant to replace us."

Crystal says, "So go ahead and replace us. He doesn't have to *kill* us. Why the drama?"

"Maybe it *is* drama. Colony footage is shown on TV. Maybe colonists won't accept mechs unless they see them fighting alongside the Rangers."

Ivan says, "We could come up with dozen theories. Question is, do we believe Li'l Mike's story?"

When Junior Rangers nod sad agreement, Ivan sighs heavily, "Me too. Next question, what do we do about it?"

I point to Li'l Mike and run a hand across my throat. Crystal says, "You don't want to compare his files with Segundo's?"

"There's no point now. Li'l Mike knows that we know about the project. He can't be allowed to pass on that information."

The mech doesn't flinch when Anacine reaches out a hand to flip the switch on his neck. As Li'l Mike's pistons freeze in place, Anacine says, "It's just cruel talking about this in front of his face."

Siff says, [Save your sympathy for us. Blaitel is trying to kill us and there's nothing we can do about it.]

I say, "We can kill the mechs first."

[That would get suspicious after a while.]

"Then we kill Blaitel."

Junior Rangers are desperate enough to consider the possibility. Ivan says, "It would have to be before one of us goes for counseling session. Doc Blaitel will discover our plans from Interrogator."

Crystal says, "We don't know how detailed that information gets, but your point is taken. We're helpless to lie under the Interrogator. Doc Blaitel will find out that we know his plans. He'll erase that knowledge from our heads and once again we'll be target dummies for his mechs."

Junior Rangers fall into depressed silence. It seems the whole universe is against us. I say, "It comes back to killing Blaitel."

Ivan says, "Project couldn't have originated with Blaitel. Ranger administrators would just replace him. They might bring in someone worse."

Anacine thumbs to the window. "Well, mates. Klondike-2 wouldn't be such a bad place to settle down."

After we decide that this mission will be our last, it feels like a great weight has been lifted. Klondike-5 will be our permanent home. Junior Rangers smile and slap giddy high fives. We don't even discuss it much. There's no other option. Whatever Doc Blaitel does to keep us coming back isn't working. Maybe the fact that it's Blaitel trying to kill us.

Anacine points to Li'l Mike's still form. "What about our mate? Down to the swamp?"

I say, "Iguanas might find it and bring him back. Wipe the memory first."

Crystal drags Li'l Mike by the foot to the lab in back. "I'll fry his chips to carbon."

"Sounds like a religious ceremony."

"Call it an exorcism."

In the morning we toss the mech's body over the platform, minus data registers. We mix his data chips with acid to make fertilizer for our farm. Anacine says, "Why don't we explore a few of the reefs? It'll be easier to skip out on the recall."

Siff says, [Your leg, Thuy. You won't be able to swim.]

"I guess I could bear sitting in the doorway. As long as there's a hot sun and I don't have to watch out for alligators."

Crystal winks at Ivan. "What do you think, mon? Could you talk Terra into a survey of the reefs? I hear she's got a killer bikini."

"Where scientific knowledge is of concern, just try to stop her."

We get permission to explore the island reefs. Lieutenant Nofree could care less about us. With my new information he's busy with colonists building a new world in the trees.

Parked outside a small island, trees don't rise two kilometers into the air like they do on the big landmasses, but they're still a hundred meters tall. On an expedition inland Crystal and Siff find a band of iguanas. They back out, not risking adverse contact. With new civilian lives awaiting us, Junior Rangers are cautious. No one wants to die in the last week before retirement.

We spend the day fishing or playing in the water. Terra does indeed have a killer bikini. We don't discuss out loud our plan to miss recall. Ivan will ask Terra to join us just before the Event. The rest of us are completely against the idea, even if Ivan drops us off first, risking only his own neck. With only that one small detail clouding the future, Doc Blaitel calls through the Dragonfly's radio, "Siff, I'd like to see you for a session."

We back away as if spidery hands could reach through the speaker grill. Adding stuttering to the lisp, Siff says, "Ith... ith... ith thith about Li'l Mike? We told you he fell off the platform."

"You *told* me?" Doc Blaitel says perceptively. "No, it's not about Li'l Mike."

"We're kind of bithy out here."

"I'll expect you tomorrow. Blaitel, out."

Ivan says, "Terra, could you excuse us?"

"Going to make your little conspiracies?" Charlie First winks.

When we don't move, Terra says, "Fine. I'm going swimming. Join me when you're done."

Ivan nods and no one says a thing until the hatch is closed. I say, "Do you think it's really about Li'l Mike?"

Siff snaps, [Of course it is! I'm screwed.]

Crystal says, "We all are. You'll give away the whole plan, no offense."

[Why me? Blaitel could have picked anyone.]

"Weakest link." Crystal holds up a metal hand. "Sorry. Is there any chance we could run away?"

Ivan says, "Rangers would be pleased to track us down halfway around world. I'm sure of that much."

Anacine says, "Maybe you air-breathers. I could lose myself in the ocean."

Crystal says, "We could split up and bury ourselves in the swamp."

I say, "Let's not panic. What if Siff went in to see Doc Blaitel?"

Ivan speaks slowly as if to a child, "We already said why that can't happen."

"What if Siff doesn't know anything? What if Siff saw Li'l Mike fall off the platform like we said? Crystal, you still have the Interrogator programs we took from Blaitel, right? We could adjust Siff's memories. Smooth things out as it were."

[No one is going to smooth *my* mind! You'd smooth me into a milkshake.]

"Would you rather Doc Blaitel did it, or us?"

Crystal says, "It doesn't matter. We got the software but we don't got the hardware."

"You took apart the Interrogator on Uridie-3. Could you put together another one?"

"I took notes." Crystal puts on pogs to run through the Dragonfly's inventory, "A bunch of transistors and relays, miniature radio transmitters, antennas... the construction wouldn't be difficult. Just time consuming."

Siff says, [I didn't agree to anything.]

Ivan says, "Executive decision. Your mind *will* be clean one way or another. Crystal, you got two days. Dragonfly is going rogue."

Crystal piles equipment on the lab bench in back. Ivan goes out to keep Terra away while Siff, Anacine, and I do whatever bits we can to help. Doc Blaitel's Interrogator is about the size of a loaf of bread. Crystal's looks more like a suitcase made with a child's erector set. We'll be lucky if Siff's head doesn't catch on fire.

We can't keep Terra away forever. We have a picnic dinner outside but she insists on sleeping on a cot indoors. When she steps back to the kitchen area, Terra squints at the growing pile of circuits. "Hey, Crystal, what are you making? A model roller coaster?"

"Homework assignment. I'm building an eight-bit parallel computer."

Terra looks back at us and shrugs. "Glad I'm out of school."

Junior Rangers sigh inwardly. It looks as if Terra will be cool. We'll see what she does when we refuse a direct order to return. Hopefully it will never come to that. Doc Blaitel sometimes gets busy with emergencies.

Crystal sleeps two hours that night and is hard at work the next morning. The main structure of the Interrogator is in place but there are hundreds of chips to wire. As we get breakfast to take outside, Terra says, "What's with the marathon session? I'll tell Nofree to ease up."

Ivan leads her away by the arm. "We find it better to be inconspicuous."

"Maybe that's the problem, you're too inconspicuous. You're not out there making friends."

"Da, that's our problem," Ivan agrees, shutting the hatch on the way out.

I say to Crystal, "How much longer?"

"Another day at least, if it even works."

Eating bricko meekly on his cot, Siff doesn't say anything. Maybe we should handcuff him to his bunk before Siff runs. Doc Blaitel calls at noon, "Siff, I thought I'd hear from you by now. Did you forget our appointment?"

"We were coming later thith afternoon," Siff lies, stalling for time.

"I'm changing that to ASAP. I'll inform Ivan. Blaitel, out."

Siff moans, "I'm thcrewed," a few times before coding to Ivan swimming outside with Anacine and Terra.

Ivan says, [I can claim engine problem. That might get us to tomorrow.]

I code, [I'm not sure we can put him off this time. Blaitel is excited about something. He might send the Widow.]

Anacine says, [So let's make a real excuse. Ivan can crash the Dragonfly gently in the canopy. By the time they dig us out, Crystal will be finished and Siff will be as pure and innocent as a lamb.]

[Baaaa!]

[Jets are busted, we couldn't run from Black Widow if we tried. I guess we have no other choice but to crash. Okay, we're coming back in.]

As we buckle into our seats, Terra walks forward from the hold pointing a blaster. "Sorry, mates, I got orders. You will each handcuff yourselves to your seats. I'll pilot the Dragonfly."

Doc Blaitel must suspect that we plan to miss recall. Terra tosses plastic handcuffs to each of us, and as we slowly put them on, there's a knocking from inside a cabinet. Terra takes the safety off. "Who's that?"

No one says anything. When the knocking sounds again, Terra says, "Li'l Mike? You said he fell into the swamp. No wonder Blaitel's mad."

We look sheepishly at the cabinet. Suspecting a trick, Terra steadies the blaster and keeps one eye on us as she turns the handle. The door flies open as disembodied arms and legs spring into the room like hungry zombies. While Terra falls away screaming, I remove her blaster, and toss it to Siff. Crystal's limbs fall dead to the floor. "I could only program them for that one jump."

Siff points the blaster to the hatch. [It was enough. Get out, Terra.]

Terra looks at Ivan. "Sweetie?"

"You pointed blaster first. Out."

She turns to Siff. "You wouldn't really shoot a Ranger."

Anacine takes the blaster. "I would."

When Terra doesn't move, the blaster barks once leaving a barb embedded in the shoulder near her gills. "What do you say, Charlie First? Should I turn on the juice?"

"You're dead," Terra says, wincing and heading for the door.

Crystal clips the taser wire with a steel finger before the hatch closes. "Glad that was you, mon, and not me."

"We're not going back, right? Besides, I've wanted to do that for a long time. Thinks she's so great."

As Crystal locks the door, Ivan says, "I'm cutting radio transmitter. Terra can't call Blaitel but this changes everything. Rangers will be coming after us. There's no way to stay on Klondike without fight."

Crystal says, "A fight we could never win. So what do we do?"

[I guess the Interrogator plan is out.]

I say, "Now that we've gone rogue, Blaitel won't stop with Siff. If we're caught, he's going to scan all of us. He'll know we destroyed Li'l Mike. He'll know we planned to run. He'll know that we know he programmed Li'l Mike to kill us."

Ivan says, "What do you suggest?"

"We continue building the Interrogator. For each of us we erase knowledge of our plans. We erase knowledge of Li'l Mike's treachery. Blaitel won't find a thing in our heads."

Crystal says, "We go back to the moon like sheep? Doc Blaitel will send another Li'l Mike after us."

"Not quite. We record everything we know right now in a journal. Then we erase our memories. When we get back to the moon, we'll read our notes in our own hand, and we can figure out what to do then."

Junior Rangers don't want something scraping around inside our brains, but we don't know what else to do. Getting away from the Rangers was always a long shot. Siff thumbs to the window. "What about Terra?"

Anacine says, "We were careful. She can't tell Blaitel anything."

I say, "She pulled a blaster on us, we kicked her out. That's what she'll tell Blaitel. That's what Doc Blaitel will find in our heads."

Ivan guns the engine. "If we don't make it, it's been honor to serve with all of you." We wave at Terra as the Dragonfly lifts off and floats away over the sea. "Where to? Black Widow will be after us within hour."

Crystal says, "Dive for the deep ocean. We should be able to hide long enough to finish the Interrogator."

"One more thing," Ivan says, thumbing the radio. "Doc Blaitel, this is Ivan. Because you had Terra hold blaster on us, Junior Rangers are on strike. We'll be back before recall. Trans Luna Corp will hear about this outrage."

When the radio clicks off, Anacine says, "You think that will hold them?"

I say, "They'll be careful if they come after us. Their secret project would die alongside the Junior Rangers."

We make neural maps of each of us with Doc Blaitel's software and Crystal's Interrogator. After recording diaries, we gently scrape memories free of conspiracy. We make one more stop before returning to the Homestead. Siff climbs down to retrieve the mech's body, and hauls it to the platform. We set him near the edge with a rake in his hands. With Junior Rangers watching, I pull a string to topple Li'l Mike over the edge. We all saw it, just like we said. If Doc Blaitel searches our memories we'll each have an image of Li'l Mike's fall.

There's no armed guard waiting when we return. Maybe Doc Blaitel really is worried about our reporting him. We get our first sign that things may be all right when Terra sticks her head through the belly hatch. "Ivan! Where have you been, sweetie? I've been lonely."

Ivan says, "Um, did you have session with Doc Blaitel recently?"

"I went yesterday as a matter of fact. Why?"

"No reason. Could you excuse us for little bit."

"Well," she pouts. "Don't take too long."

There are gaps in our memories, and gaps as to why there are gaps, but we don't want to say too much before Siff goes to see Doc Blaitel. That fact we do remember. Anacine says, "Were we really thinking about missing recall?"

I say, "You want me to check my notes?"

A look of concentration on his face, Siff says, [Don't. I'm going to see Blaitel. Talk later.]

His mind studiously blank, Siff is as prepared for this test as for any in his life. This time he'll only pass for what he doesn't know. When Siff climbs down through the hatch, Crystal says, "I remember we were mad enough to stay on Klondike-2. The reasons escape me. If we do get through these next few days I'm not sure I want to get that anger back."

Ivan says, "You can't stick head in sand. Survival may depend on what we wrote in diaries. There's note on cover, don't read until we're back on moon."

In the few days we were gone, colonists established relationships with tribes of iguanas. The colony biologist swears they have a complex language made up of clicks, grunts and "ooks". On day twenty-eight we wake early in the morning, eat a quick breakfast, and belt into our seats.

The final start of the engines is always a tense moment. If we fail to get airborne we'll have to scramble to get to the Black Widow in time to make the rendezvous. With my cast I'll be slower than the others.

If we miss the opening of the black hole we'll be stuck on this world forever. I guess I could stand that. Klondike-2 has everything: water, food, interesting plants, animals, and oceans. I would miss the excitement of being a Junior Ranger but there are worse places to get stuck.

The Black Widow is not far away as the Dragonfly rises. It seems like she's stalking us for some reason. We couldn't rebuild the jets but the Dragonfly is well enough to haul fuel. Ivan calls, "All systems go. Converge at rendezvous point five kilometers."

"Roger, Dragonfly. Black Widow, all systems go."

As we fly higher, the outline of the giant forested island stretches out around the Homestead anchored in her horseshoe bay. Somewhere down there in the kilometer high forest is the mech's body, lying where it fell from the platform. I guess we won't miss Li'l Mike's company. For the first few years colonists will struggle to survive and build in the forest. Eventually they'll move to the reefs and other islands beyond, an entire world to fill. It's hard to imagine such wealth. Siff mirrors my thoughts, coding, [I had half a mind to miss the recall. Did you read your diary?]

[We promised not to, remember?]

[No, I don't. Well the perfect world is out there somewhere. We'll know it when we find it, and miss that final call.]

[Or get clobbered by the beasts in between.]

At five kilometer Ivan drops the Dragonfly onto the larger Widow. After magnetic feet latch on, Ivan idles our engines. Fuel pumps into the Black Widow's tanks but we keep a small emergency reserve. If the Black Widow has sudden problems we can rev up and head us into the hole. Ivan says, "Dragonfly linked. You got the ball, Jolly."

"Roger, Dragonfly. Inversion space at T-minus ten minutes."

Jolly takes us higher to ten kilometers. We're early but when you're talking interstellar jumps, one second late means never. We circle the area chatting about school assignments. Klondike-2 is already part of our past.

We start to fall. The Black Widow transmits a radio beacon as the black hole appears beneath us. I take one last look at the forest wondering where those iguanas took our light poles, and the forest blinks out, replaced by the rough rock floor of our lunar cavern.

The Black Widow has plenty of time to slow and land gently on the floor. I forget how big the Lunar Transfer Station is when there's no colony ship inside. Long and short arise from comparison. I think about saying that out loud but Siff's been frustrated enough. Ivan turns off our engines and we shake hands all around.

Anacine says, "Another fine mission, mates. Very few casualties."

I knock on my cast. "And this will be off in plenty of time for the next."

Siff says, [And Ivan's broken nose will heal into the proper shape for a gargoyle.]

Ivan rubs his nose. "I'm surprised Crystal didn't win any new linked parts. You getting cautious in old age?"

"I got gator teeth in my ankle. Doesn't that count?"

"At least you got replacement legs to finish chores."

Crystal looks blank.

"Did you forget bet? The colonists landed on water as I predicted. You've got ship to wash, and make sure you get all bugs out of grill."

Siff says, [Don't sweat it, Crystal. I did a little programming at the reef.]

A disjointed collection of Crystal's arms and legs crawl out of the closet dragging a bucket and sponge. Siff says, [I built my own mech to replace Li'l Mike. It's got the scrubbing part down but I hope it doesn't snap an antenna.]

"You keep that monstrosity away from paint."

Crystal stands up, linked parts humming smoothly with hidden power. "You calling me a monster?"

I say, "Come on guys, leave Ivan alone. He's not such a bad guy." Possessing frugality, one can be generous.

Siff says, [You defend him after the way he was riding you?]

"He was right about some things. Watch." I think about the courage of Lefty and Half-tusk in the freezing swamp. While the others squirm uncomfortably, I push a needle slowly through the pad of my index finger.

Anacine winces. "Thuy, stop it."

Ivan scoffs, "We've seen that trick, Gravitol takes away pain."

I hold out my bare wrist. "I lost my leech, remember? You were right, Ivan. Pain doesn't come in a bottle. It's in the mind and you can train the mind to ignore it."

I pull the bloody needle out, and flip it into the trashcan. I rise and head for the exit leaving the others staring open-mouthed behind me. Maybe I'm growing up, maybe I'm not, but I won't let Ivan get to me. I'll do what *I* think is right. I'll make my own mistakes, I'll learn, and I'll stay alive. After all those others have passed away, I'm still alive. As I walk through the corridor, I put the small notebook in my pocket, wondering what's the big secret.

Doc Blaitel brings two cups of coffee to Captain Wallen's office, and sets them on her desk. Without asking, the Ranger Captain adulterates each with a finger of clear liquid. She takes a gulp, wincing. "So what did the scans show?"

Doc Blaitel sips judiciously. "Just what they said, Li'l Mike fell off the platform."

"You don't believe it?"

"Five people watching the exact same thing? The scans are too consistent, too perfect."

"So they've mastered mind control."

"Not exactly. If what I suspect is true, Junior Rangers have advanced far beyond what I thought possible. They'll begin to do all the hard work of the project without our help."

"So the Junior Rangers don't have to die?"

"On the contrary. When they see what's coming, they'll realize that killing themselves is the only way to proceed."

"I just hope they don't take us with them."

Doc Blaitel rubs his glasses with a shirt. "I wouldn't worry about that, Harveen. If the Junior Rangers make a mistake, they'll take the whole species down with them."

Excerpt from Book 6: Crabb World

Episode 1 – The Joust

Hermann floats in the algae fringe around the island town of Manse. He pumps filter mesh at his neck, eating microscopic zooplankton while waiting for his friend Trichelle to make her way from the tidal pools. Pincers clamp onto a tubular metal frame of the town while jumper feet troll the water, stirring nutrients into an upwelling current towards his mouth.

A thousand meters offshore from Cork, Manse receives industrial runoff from the Lowage River. Hermann barely notices the taint, having lived all his life among slum tidal pools. He's lucky to even get a spot in the town school. Most of the crabbs in his cohort crawl inland to factory schools.

Hearing the horn of the ferry preparing to leave port, Hermann looks once more to Cork and ducks under the algae fringe. Hermann flutters limbs and snaps mid-crease for power, heading for the underwater entrance to Manse Preparatory School. With gills as well as lungs, crabbs breathe just as easily underwater as in air.

Corridors are packed. Crabbs swing pincers as they fight their way to class. *Save it for the joust*, Hermann thinks in dismay. When a feeder hand pinches, Hermann swings to shred the offender. His friend Reggie let's go, luminescent patches on his

cheeks flashing mock fear, "Don't disembowel
me!"

"Oh, shut up."

"Serves you right for looking four ahead."

Hermann's eyestalks had all been
concentrating on the classroom entrance, a crabb's
great focus. He keeps one on Reggie, two ahead,
and one facing backwards looking for Trichelle.
"How can you be so calm on this of all days?"

"It doesn't really matter when you're
destined for the labor pool."

"If I were assigned to labor, I'd just head for
open ocean."

"Two days without the polychum and you'd
come crawling back."

"The sea is full of eel and fish, my friend."

Hermann swims ahead and turns into a
classroom. He takes his companion from a half
empty rack, slipping pincers and feeder arms up
through the body. He pulls the tube down
comfortably around his upper shell, flashing,
"Testing, testing."

He checks light repeaters on the front hood.
Charged and ready to go, Hermann calls up the
day's news to check with two bent eyes. His others
scan the room for Krunch or Trichelle. The bullies
Chron and Mikal bounce off the far wall. Jets on
their companions drive like tugboats in his
direction. Sensing his alarm, the companion says,
"Hermann, shall I call a teacher?"

"No!" Hermann chirps. He is no scared
nymph.

Their cheeks flash malice. Hermann braces for a hard knock, and then a miracle. Trichelle swims in the door clacking loudly. Hermann practically rips a pincer out, churning to get out of Mikal's path. He feels both elated and shamed at avoiding a fight. Chancing one eye back, emotions dance through the bully's photospheres as well.

Hermann meets Trichelle at the companion rack. With a rare third crease, she is considered a beauty among crabbs. They're joined by Reggie and Krunch, swimming in with the last bell. Trichelle says, "Last week in this squid trap, boys."

Krunch puts meaty claws on both Reggie and Hermann's backs. "It was the best of times," he says emotionally. "And one more grand joust to remember them all."

Hermann says, "Don't you think it a little barbaric sending an entire cohort out onto the rock with weapons?"

Reggie's cheeks color disapproval, "It's tradition. Besides, how would they decide who to send to the Spring Festival?"

Hermann shrugs feeder arms, not wanting to continue a discussion he would lose. Crabbs are nothing if not set in their ways. Drumming a jumper in front, the teacher calls class to order. Amid a last flurry of securing companions, students line up to squeal a song and get instructions for the day. The teacher, Sou Plank, says, "And so we emerge on the tide of a new age..."

Hermann flashes dimly, "Can you believe this fish is on my triune?"

Reggie says, "Mine too, and he doesn't like me half as much as you."

Krunch says, "You're both on stream for good jobs. What choice have I got?" There is something pleading in Krunch's voice. He has a monoploid's need for validation, but anything they say would sound insincere.

Trichelle saves them, waving a pincher high. "Sou Plank, are final projects due today?"

Speech interrupted, Sou Plank clacks several times. It's an embarrassing reflex that they assume sent the poor crabb into teaching. Pale green shell unscuffed by pik or hard work, Sou Plank shows all the more enthusiasm for the violent games of others. "Surely you joke, mon Trichelle! The joust! The joust! Final projects can be presented during tribulations. I'm sure all of you will be recommended for apprenticeships or upper academies."

As Sou Plank's eyestalks sweep the ranks, one or two linger sadly on Krunch. Millions of ovoids unite in spawning but always a few escape to grow with one set of chromosomes – clones. Identical to parent crabb, monoploids lack the potential of new genetic strengths from combination.

Sensitive to slights, Krunch shrinks in his shell. "I'll show him," he colors.

After Sou Plank dismisses students to work, the friends swim to Reggie's project in the corner, a racer with turbo jets and fins. Reggie pulls a rag from a compartment in his companion, rubbing vigorously at metal welds. "These will have to be ground and buffed," he says, turning an eye pointedly to Trichelle.

"I have my own project, and a few last adjustments before lunch."

Hermann says, "Your sculptures are back home."

"Not those." Her cheeks twinkle mischievously, "I made presents for all of you."

Krunch waves pincers at his sides. "I know! I know! I saw them last week!"

"Calm down, Krunch. You agreed to keep quiet."

"I didn't say anything!"

While Trichelle swims to a locker, Reggie and Hermann exchange glances. Hermann signals quietly, "What is it, Krunch?"

Krunch keeps three eyes nervously on Trichelle's back while tapping his chest plate repeatedly with a mid-limb. "What does that mean?" Reggie flashes brightly.

Trichelle snaps pincers at Krunch while she swims back with a bundle. "I didn't say anything!" Krunch complains.

"I know, calm down. I made one for you too." Trichelle passes out shiny material garments of interlocked rings. "Chainmail," she says proudly. "For the joust. Guaranteed to turn back the sharpest pik."

Reggie dangles his in front of him for fit. "It's beautiful, Trichelle. When did you have time?"

"Here and there I picked up scraps to weld at night. I hope they fit."

Krunch already has the companion off, pulling chainmail over his shell. "It's loose."

"You'll have leather underneath, dummy. Rings spread out the impact."

As Reggie and Hermann try theirs on for fit, Mikal jets by squealing, "Hah! You look like a bunch of junk cans!"

Trichelle looks hurt, but to be honest, Hermann thinks, metal rings run the gamut of size and coloring. Chainmail on the optilock sparkles like the scales of a sunfish. Hermann would like to put his quietly away. Reggie spins, slamming a mailed pincer onto Mikal's skull ridge. As the crabb drifts to the floor, Reggie flashes warmly, "It works! I hardly felt that, Trichelle. Thanks!"

Trichelle beams again. "Well, I'll tighten the flaps before jousting. I had to guess your measurements."

An angry Sou Plank swims over to see what the commotion is. Seeing chainmail and Mikal's twitching limbs, he sizes it up accurately. Hermann thinks Reggie's in trouble, but Sou Plank only says, "Save some for the rock, gentlemen," and swims away with averted eyestalks.

The lunchroom in Manse Preparatory School has flaps at the entrance to hold algae and zooplankton pumped in from the fringe outside, but it's not enough to sustain a growing crabb. For complete dietary needs, lunch workers sell eel, fish, and squid in seaweed wraps. Hermann and friends seldom have rings for such treats. They rely instead on charitable handouts of polychum provided by the school.

Hermann waits in line to receive his allotment in a reusable rubber sheet. For him there's no delicious seaweed wrap for dessert. When they gather to eat near the wall, Hermann notices how Krunch kept his companion on. Some of the other students have theirs as well, but they're reading or watching videos on the inset optilock. Krunch is quiet, scrunched partway into the tube.

Hermann blinks to Trichelle, who says, "What do you got there, Krunch?"

Luminescent patches on Krunch's cheeks flash, "Nothing." Because he usually clacks, they know immediately Krunch's mouth must be full. It's not the untouched polychum pack in Krunch's mid-limb.

Reggie tips the companion to look down inside. "He's eating! What do you got? Is that eel?"

Krunch's cheeks color embarrassment as he mumbles, "I've got to keep my strength for the joust."

As they rotate Krunch's companion back and forth to work him loose, Hermann says, "I've got to joust too."

"No one expects you to do well," Krunch says unkindly, albeit, truthfully.

Trichelle says, "Come on, Krunch. Give us a bite!"

With Krunch separated from companion and spinning away, he finally relents. "Just a piece, the cave mother gave it to me for luck."

The miserly pinch of eel is only enough to remind them how bad the polychum is. "Thanks," Hermann clacks sarcastically. "I'll guard your back real well, partner."

When the others grow quiet, Hermann says, "Krunch?"

The big crabb doesn't say anything. Reggie says, "Hermann, you know how you and Krunch have always been partners?"

"Yeah?" Hermann says, getting a funny feeling. Although they never go far in competition, Krunch has saved him many an injury.

"We decided we might change partners this time. Krunch and I, you and Trichelle."

"You all decided this?" Hermann says, the blushing photospheres of his friends confirming a conspiracy.

"Why?" he says. "Krunch? Trichelle?"

Krunch stays quiet. Trichelle says, "I wanted to, Hermann. We're best friends."

"Yeah, but... We always... I always..."

"It was me, Hermann," Krunch says. His normally calm voice is forceful. "It's the tribulations. You got electronics. Trichelle has art. What do I have? I'm just a big dumb half-wit."

"No, Krunch," he says, but Krunch hasn't finished.

"I thought that I might win the joust if Reggie was my partner. My triune might see."

Hermann waves feeder arms uncertainly. Everything Krunch says is true. The crabb is a powerful jouster. Hermann is mortified to realize he's been holding his friend back. All he's thinking about is saving his own shell. Hermann says slowly, "Okay, Krunch. You're right. I've carried you long enough."

Trichelle colors amusement, wrapping a pincer around Hermann's shell. "That's the spirit. We'll show them how it's done."

Yes, we'll show them. And you've given me a nice coat of mail to buy your guilt if we don't.

Overseeing developments, Mikal and Chron flash humor and slap at each other in hysterics. From the safety of distance, Mikal shines,

> "Hermann, Hermann, lost his shell.
> Sand fleas biting where you dwell."

As Reggie braces jumpers against the wall, Mikal and Chron look down and get busy with lunch. Hermann puts a mid-limb out. "We'll have our chance on the rock."

The end of term joust is a tradition all over Creche, not just Manse Preparatory. Schools herd students to open rock to batter each other with cold steel implements: pik, mallet, cable, and blocker. The designs haven't changed since ancient times.

Hermann pulls a rusted pik from the pile, wondering if their P.E. equipment doesn't date to ancient times. Tapping blunted point on rock, Hermann detects a crack somewhere along the shaft. He just goes with it, shuffling along to find a spot near the edge. Others are waiting and Hermann has no plans to put the weapon to test.

Chainmail sparkling, Trichelle follows Hermann to the edge with a blocker. Looking down into the water, she says, "Not here, partner. One good whack and we're out."

Hermann says defensively, "This is where Krunch and I always stand. We do okay."

"You standing behind him, and Krunch taking all comers. Not this time, buddy. Into the middle. I'll sweep the blocker and you come in behind to run them through."

"With this?" Hermann says incredulously.

"You know what I mean. Bonk 'em on the ridge or poke them over."

"You really like this stupid ritual, don't you?"

Three beautiful plates rising and falling as she breathes, Trichelle says, "We're crabbs, Hermann! Masters of the world, and it all starts here!" Trichelle twirls, swinging blocker back and forth like a scythe.

"I don't think our barbarian ancestors were as grand as you sculpt them. Giant squid owned the seas. Birds dominated land. Crabbs could only hide in tide pools. Even now the lowly mudfish gobble more nymphs than ever have a chance to grow."

Trichelle waves it away. "That's just housekeeping. We could save the nymphs if we wanted, but where would we put them all?" She cracks the blocker with a pincer. "This reminds us where we came from, born into a violent world."

Hermann flashes for Krunch and Reggie, "Over here!"

Krunch wields his signature weapon, a mallet. Reggie has a pik and throwing cable. As they face each other, Hermann says hopefully, "Team?"

Reggie says, "Only two can win. If we're the last, will you jump?"

"Absolutely," Hermann flashes.

Trichelle says slyly, "Why don't we discuss that when the time comes?"

Krunch flashes agreeably, but Reggie says, "Remember why we're doing this."

Trichelle looks at Krunch, "Oh yeah. I'll go down, but Reggie, could you at least give me a push? I don't want to look like a coward." She stares at Hermann with one eye back as she crawls towards the middle of the rock to size up the competition.

The battlefield is a tabletop rock polished flat and rising sheer a meter out of the ocean. It seems as if the whole town floats in boats around the tiny, floating island, ready to pull out losers and feed them a consolation feast. *"At least there's that,"* Hermann thinks. Not all traditions are foolish.

All too soon, teachers crawl onto their barge and push off. The wary, bewildered cohort looks around instinctively for cracks to hide in. A ringing bell signals the start. Unofficially, enemies outside the joust have been planning maneuvers for several minutes. Before the last note fades, aggrieved crabbs charge over the rock with lowered lances. Heavy mallets are drawn back, blockers braced.

Many like Hermann are usually willing to go over the edge without a fuss. In this, the big one, even the weakest is prepared to trade blows. Hermann turns his back to Trichelle and readies the pik like a club. Four eyes twirl on stalks looking desperately for danger. In the middle of the rock, that seems to include every direction. *Curse Trichelle.* Not everyone abides the mercy rule. After being knocked over it's unlikely he would be pummeled, but near an edge he could roll off quickly.

A crabb smaller than Hermann named Porge charges with a mallet. Two emotions rush to Hermann's cheeks, relief that the potential damage is small, and outrage that the little crabb would think Hermann a manageable foe. Hermann aims the pik and slams down with a satisfying crack. Hit on the skull ridge, Porge's eyestalks go limp. The crabb keels over, legs paddling aimlessly.

Watching with a back eye, Trichelle says, "Nice!"

Overly proud of himself, Hermann nudges Porge with a jumper. "Do you yield?"

"Yes, of course," Porge squeals. As the defeated crabb scuttles off low, Porge flashes, "Good shot. I'll look for you in the boats."

For a fraction of a second Hermann raises upper shell in challenge. *In the boats? What if I win?* Of course it is only vanity. To his left, Krunch swings mallet back and forth like a broom, sweeping crabbs across the rock with each mighty pass. Reggie runs behind, poling stunned crabbs into the water without even requesting yield. There isn't time.

Hearing a squeal, Hermann looks back. Chron has Trichelle's pincer caught in a cable, pulling her off balance. Trichelle slams her blocker hard on the rock trying to right herself. As Mikal scuttles in behind with a pik, Hermann looks for help. Where is the team?

Hermann's chainmail flashes in the sun. Through a roaring in his ears, Hermann realizes this could be a defining moment in his life. He's no hero but luck sides with the little guy sometimes. Hermann lowers the pik. Too scared to aim for a vulnerable spot, Hermann just runs.

With four eyes, it's all but impossible to sneak up on a crabb. Mikal lets Hermann get close before turning to parry Hermann's pik easily with his own. Hermann barrels into Mikal, hoping to at least knock his pik away. It's a legal, but frowned upon, "grab and chuck". Mikal holds tight to his pik.

With luminescent patches flashing triumph, he brings up a metal barb in a mid-limb. A hundred volts spread over Hermann's mail like a lightning bolt. Limbs twitching, Hermann realizes he was the target all along. Trichelle was just being pulled out of the way. "*Illegal*," Hermann thinks as he goes down. *Illegal.*

Cold rock jumps up to smash his cheek. It's the last thing Hermann remembers until a bucket of seawater pours over his head from a father in a boat. "A sparker," Hermann clacks incoherently. He tries to justify his miraculous appearance in the loser's boat. "Mikal had a sparker."

Not listening, the father flashes humor again, pouring another bucket until Hermann jumps up and scuttles to the edge in annoyance. Only four combatants remain on the rock, Krunch and Reggie among them. The crowd cheers. Mikal and Chron cheer as well from their vantage point, firmly in control of a teacher on the official barge. At least their cheating has been detected.

For all his disdain of the sport, Hermann watches as eagerly as the rest. He looks belatedly for his partner. Just climbing into a fishing boat two over, Hermann waves and Trichelle waves back. She must have been last off, Hermann thinks, wondering if she jumped. If Trichelle was last, she survived long after he had gone down. Probably no one wanted to bash that pretty shell, Hermann thinks sourly.

The crowd gasps as Krunch's mallet swings high over the head of a ducking Stantin. Stantin and Pell are not among the biggest of the cohort but they're smart and fast. Hermann isn't surprised to see them at the end. Reggie's cable flashes through the air, distracting the pair as Krunch lumbers closer for the kill. Pell trips. Reggie charges with pik as Stantin bends to pull him up. The crowd flashes excitement as Stantin dives to the side revealing Pell's pik firmly planted and aimed for Reggie's chest plate.

"It's a fake!" Hermann sends with the rest, heart hammering in his throat.

Surely Trichelle's chainmail will be no match. Reggie's charge is as fake as Pell's fall. Pulling up short, Reggie's cable is already wrapped around the rolling Stantin's right thumper. Reggie spins, sending Stantin on a new trajectory rolling over the edge, cable and all. As quickly as that, Krunch stands over Pell, mallet held high. "Do you yield?" he says warmly.

"Are you kidding?" Pell says, flashing warmly back.

On Creche's airless moon Imarron, a ten-year female named Lina decorates her upper chest plate with dyes from a small makeup net. She is alone inside the compartment of a personal transport that bounces across the surface of the moon like a silver shell scraping across red powder. Lenses show flat, empty land ahead all the way to low hills in the distance. Lina switches the screen to an optilock romance.

She came to the moon for adventure, but lately it's a succession of one-night shows in small towns all over Imarron. Two nights are even worse. She has to spend a day making small talk with miners and farmers. The transport slows, announcing, "Krumpfl Deep. Where would you like to be delivered?"

Lina switches the opti to an outside view. A line of buildings is built directly into the hill. Further down the road there are a few structures that are little more than alcoves or tractor ramps leading into the ground. As on most of the airless moon, crabbs dig businesses and homes into the safety of the rock. "The Foggy Goon, I believe," Lina says, trying to recall without turning on the companion.

She takes it as a good sign when the transport rolls smoothly forward and engages a public lock. The magnetic seal clicks, and the wall dissolves in rolling sheets of metal revealing a busy public walk beyond. Lina says, "Can you stick around a few hours? I plan to go back to Capsill tonight."

"Certainly. Enjoy your visit."

"Ugh, I'll try." Lina pushes into a scuttling line of crabbs.

She flashes, "Can anyone tell me where the Goon is?" Males crowd around offering escort.

In the small town, Lina knows she is more attractive for the novelty of a new shell than she is as potential mate. Still, the attention is nice, and the owner will invite her back if she brings new customers.

In a cluster of red, white, and purple shells, Lina flirts and pretends interest all the way to the Foggy Goon. A few of the younger crabbs stop at the doorway, too nervous or intimidated to come inside. Lina is happy to see many follow. The owner greets her and offers menus to the males, driving off a few more. Lina says, "What time do crabbs get off work?"

The large male checks a wrist companion. "In about fifteen minutes. You can start the show and I'll put a couple of sweepers outside. This place fills up fast."

Lina looks around the dimly lit cave filled with eating rocks and a few diners. The Foggy Goon serves regular food as well as the fermented fish parts of a sour bar. She says, "Bouncers?"

The owner snaps work-scarred pincers. "Never need 'em. This is a nice quiet town."

"We'll see." Lina crawls over to add her chip to the synthesizer. The high energy of her show never fails to stimulate a few fights. She could tone it down but the polyploid in her prefers strong reactions.

As regular patrons crawl in, Lina squeals a few old favorites to warm her voice. It gives crabbs time to order food or drinks. As rough miners with dusty shells trickle in, she dances and sings. Lina identifies where the trouble will come from, both by customer volume and number of sour fish parts consumed.

Locals are poor, with unadorned shells. Few rings hang on their mid-limbs. Miners are wealthier, showing paint and artistic shell etchings beneath the dust. One flashy crabb with a shell of cadmium yellow will either throw or receive the first swing, Lina predicts, and she is rarely wrong.

Lina sings faster songs, encouraging patrons to the small floor. Dancing to a driving hypnotic beat, Lina feels the mood of the entire room change. Isolated groups melt into one hungry cohort, heating to the sounds of her voice.

Giving the owner his money's worth, Lina keeps them dancing long minutes. They throw down fish parts to break final barriers of reserve. When the pulsing rhythm has nowhere else to go, Lina dances over to cadmium yellow and a group of locals. That is all it takes. Energy turns so quickly to violence, crabbs themselves are surprised to find that the flailing pincers they see are their own. Lina slides smoothly away as friends break up the fights.

Lina dances and twirls in ecstasy. She's ready to put on a quieter song to cool tempers and allow muttered apologies among pugilists. It's all part of the experience Lina provides, but before the first notes of her decelerant can play, a strange looking metal transport rolls through the doors. Lina leaps over the rock bar as the machine grabs fighters in snaking claws. Patrons are nonplussed as crabbs are dragged outside. Lina extends eyes above the rock, turning one to the server. "What is that?"

"It's called a Peace Shield. The government sent it last month to keep order."

"Never heard of it," Lina says. "And I'm from Capsill."

"Supposedly they're trying them out in small towns to work out the logic."

"So what are crabbs going to do if they can't let off steam?"

The server shrugs feeders and crawls off to refill bowls. It's a Triumvirate idea, Lina thinks. Most crabbs don't worry about the occasional cracked shell or severed eyestalk.

On a distant planet, mistakes are common in the early days of radio. One in particular changes the fates of two worlds. A German technician on the battlefields of France powers a transmitter thousands of times stronger than needed for relaying information to Berlin.

Lieutenant Hans Blaitel of the German First Army ducks his face in mud as British artillery shells land around him. They would not be firing unless they planned to attack. Hans plugs his ears in the hour before dawn. The fog at least keeps away spotting planes. They're firing blind.

Hans reviews the map inside his head for the hundredth time. In the panic of retreat it would not do to run in the wrong direction. The 236th Reserve Regiment holds the tram line north of Bouleaux Wood, the 235th west and the 234th inside the country village of Combles. If they're unable to hold the advance of the British Fourth Army, they're to fall back to a reinforced trench along Le Transloy, east of Morval.

The cessation of bombing brings no sense of relief. Ringing ears feel like they've been hit with bats. Surviving machine gun emplacements clack mechanically as gunners rattle belts through firing chambers to clear water and mud. Hans wishes he had a gun, but General Faulkner won't hear of it. Hans is an observer, the General's "eyes and ears" at the front while the General sleeps in a warm bed in a farmhouse in Sailly.

The charge begins with a few shouted orders. Gunfire picks up steadily and then the cries of wounded as British soldiers run into the crossed firing lines of German heavy machine guns. On tiptoes to peer over the parapet, Hans's whole body goes numb. It's the only thing that keeps him from running.

Trench warfare is a defensive tactic, hiding in deep holes to survive artillery barrages and then popping up to shoot as the enemy runs over no man's land, dying by the thousands. Counterattack follows when the attack stalls. Occasionally an attack breaks through, sending survivors scurrying back to a second trench line a hundred meters behind the first. Today there will be no counterattack. The German First is depleted by fighting in Verdun, but they still have artillery to slow the charge.

After the attack is broken, runners bring reports to Hans. Hans hops a motorcycle, riding through frozen French vineyards to Sailly. While the General and his staff review strategy, Hans eats in the kitchen. His day is not through, although Hans doesn't mind. After dinner he radio's the operational report to Berlin, and after that, he talks to Greta.

The voice of the unseen radio operator is full of concern, "Hans, it sounds so dangerous."

Nineteen years old and prone to puffing chest, Hans says, "No one can beat the German Army."

"What are these rolling iron boxes they're talking about?"

"Tanks," Hans explains patiently. "They're called tanks, but I don't think they'll be a problem. You should see them struggle through mud and craters. Easy targets for artillery. Enough of war talk. What did you have for dinner?"

"I went out with some of the girls to the Boar's Head. We shared schnitzel and spiced potatoes."

"Beer?"

"I had a sip."

"Is that what they call a mug these days?" Hans laughs. "I wish I was there."

"I heard that your division is being relieved in a few days."

"The front line division, ja. A new division comes in, and somehow I get stuck. What color are your eyes?"

"Green, Hans. You asked that before."

"Green," Hans sighs. "But I imagine also flecks of gray. Ja?"

"Maybe a bit."

"Watch out for soldiers on leave," Hans warns. "They are crazy for green eyes with flecks of gray."

"I'll be careful."

The shining sphere called Paradise City floats a kilometer in the air. Midway between the continents of Ista, Ilosta, and Nystra, Paradise City descends to the sea only once every two years during the Spring Festival.

Smaller than pinheads, millions of nymphs conceived in an artificial stream in the city's lower decks wash out into the sea. Far from land, water is nutrient poor. Hungry zooplankton are just as likely to eat nymphs as the other way around.

Caught in the current, nymphs surviving the first few days grow too big for zooplankton. Larger predators follow the current. Nymphs scatter before schools of sunfish. They sometimes find shelter in floating bits of trash.

Light-sensitive molecules accumulate in four spots on the head that eventually sprout eyestalks. The molecules react to sunlight, sending half the population deeper. They skulk in the dark, encountering squid or other carrion eaters.

It only matters that some nymphs get through. There's no relief until the current pushes into the Thousand Islands off the southern coast of Ista. Some nymphs survived in surface waters, and some in muddy trails along the sea floor.

Weeks-old nymphs are the size and shape of a peanut with eight stubby limbs, a hinge in the middle, and filter netting at the neck. Like translucent white insects they crawl onto shore to hide in the sand or tangled tree roots. Many fall prey to rats or snakes on the islands.

In the first months of life there is little thought. Cells react to stimuli from the environment. It's a mercy as so many millions are snapped up for food. Surviving nymphs grow larger, eating insects and algae. They develop more complex nervous systems, and finally thought.

"I am me," she thinks, a female nymph destined to be called the Butcher General. Destined to be called by the less grandiose name, "Pickles", the nymph observes how others around her react to the sounds of rustling leaves or splashing of water in a nearby lagoon. Immediately they scramble for safety whether it is wind, tides, or the approach of a predator. How much feeding time is wasted in fear? If they only waited a few seconds they would make better decisions.

Watching who grows fat and who gets eaten, Pickles identifies the best hiding places. She moves into a mangrove tree overhanging the water. Nymphs experiment with sound. Whistling, clicking, and snapping hardening chest plates, the familiar voices of those around her become Pickle's cohort.

They learn to cooperate to obtain food, dropping to the water to spear fish. As they get bigger they drive rats into an ambush. Some in her cohort won't eat mammals. Pickles learns to snip off the hairy coat.

With sharpening vision and lengthening eyestalks, nymphs undergo a neural growth spurt. They grow smart enough to become the creatures that dominated the world around them and colonized the moon.

Nymph cohorts make up their own names and words for things. These words are useless any time they come into contact with other cohorts. Misunderstandings lead to battles along territorial boundaries. It's a long time of testing and dislocation. Pickles' cohort is shattered and driven into the sea. With a few friends Pickles makes her way along the beach to a rocky tide pool to hide and regroup.

In the wash of the tide Pickles tastes strange chemicals. Swimming the ocean and hiking beaches, Pickles finds structures built of rock and mud. She brings friends to watch from a distance. As protective shells grow thick upon their backs, nymphs challenge each other to move closer.

They listen and watch crabbs living in the town. Grown crabbs sometimes toss them bits of fish or squid. Pickles learns quickly that not all are friendly. One of her cohort is swept up in a net. Pickles finds him later floating dead in the sea impaled on a bait hook.

A year after leaving Paradise City, photospheres on the nymph's cheeks begin dimly to glow. They see grown crabbs flashing colorfully to each other, but patterns are mysterious and nymphs have little control. Cheeks glow when they are frightened or angry. Gradually nymphs learn to control their emotions, showing color voluntarily in patterns.

Watching carefully, Pickles sees how crabbs use photospheres to talk. She mimics the patterns. When she is seen one day, a crowd of town crabbs gathers, flashing humor and throwing pieces of fish. Delighted, Pickles teaches her cohort. Soon they are out swimming next to fishing boats, flashing nonsensical patterns for food.